Whispers of the Old World
By Steven Jacobs

Whispers of the Old World

Steven Jacobs

Published by Am I Am, 2024.

WHISPERS OF THE OLD WORLD

First edition. June 15, 2024.

ISBN: 979-8227563194

Written by Steven Jacobs.

Chapter One: Danny Martin in His Workshop

As the morning fog lifted, a panoramic view of the bustling city unfolded, revealing a magnificent tableau of Victorian splendor and steampunk innovation. Tall buildings dominated the skyline, their silhouettes etched against the pale, cloud-dappled sky. Some were constructed of robust red brick, their surfaces worn by time yet exuding a steadfast, industrial charm. These structures, adorned with iron-framed windows and copper gutters, housed the heart of the city's industrious spirit.

Interspersed among these were grand edifices of ornate stonework, their facades embellished with intricate carvings and statuary. Gargoyles perched on ledges, silently overseeing the throngs below, while wrought iron balconies and balustrades lent an air of elegance to the robust architecture. The streets, a lively maze of cobblestones, thrummed with the vibrant energy of the populace.

Steam-powered carriages clattered along, their polished brass and iron exteriors gleaming in the sunlight. Overhead, dirigibles floated lazily, their vast, silken envelopes shimmering in the light. The city's transportation network, a marvel of modern engineering, seamlessly integrated elevated railways and pneumatic tubes, their tracks and pipes weaving a complex lattice above the bustling streets.

Marketplaces buzzed with activity, vendors peddling wares from wooden carts and stalls. The scent of freshly baked bread mingled with the acrid tang of coal smoke and the sweet aroma of exotic spices, creating a symphony of sensory delights. Clockwork automata, crafted with meticulous precision, moved gracefully among the crowd, assisting with various tasks and adding to the city's mechanized charm.

Street lamps, crowned with gaslit globes, stood sentinel along the thoroughfares, their soft, golden glow casting a warm, inviting light as dusk approached. In the distance, the majestic dome of the Grand Observatory rose above the skyline, its glass panels reflecting the hues of the setting sun. The observatory's aetheric telescopes, a testament to human ingenuity, pointed towards the heavens, ever seeking to unlock the mysteries of the cosmos.

Above all, the city exuded a palpable sense of progress and possibility. Its blend of Victorian grandeur and steampunk innovation painted a picture of a society on the cusp of great discoveries, where the old and the new coexisted in harmonious juxtaposition. This was a city where dreams were forged in the crucible of invention, and every street, every building, told a story of ambition and achievement.

Numerous steam-powered carriages navigate the busy streets, their chimneys emitting puffs of steam that billow into the air like miniature clouds. These carriages, a marvel of Victorian engineering, clatter along the cobblestones with a rhythmic, mechanical grace. Their exteriors are a blend of polished brass and wrought iron, adorned with intricate filigree and riveted panels that catch the sunlight, creating a dazzling display of craftsmanship.

Each carriage is a testament to the ingenuity of the city's inventors, combining the raw power of steam with the precision of clockwork mechanisms. The hissing of steam and the occasional whir of gears accompany their steady progress, adding a mechanical symphony to the city's ambient noise. Large, spoked wheels, reinforced with iron bands, turn with reliable efficiency, propelling the carriages forward through the bustling thoroughfares.

Drivers, dressed in tailored coats and top hats, expertly maneuver their vehicles, their gloved hands steady on the brass-bound steering levers. Passengers within the carriages, comfortably seated on plush, velvet-upholstered benches, peer out through glass windows etched with delicate patterns. The interiors are a blend of luxury and practicality, with brass fittings, leather straps, and polished wood panels creating an ambiance of refined elegance.

The chimneys atop these carriages, slender and elegantly curved, release rhythmic puffs of steam that rise and dissipate into the sky. This vapor, a byproduct of the powerful engines within, adds a dynamic visual element to the bustling streetscape, mingling with the morning mist and the smoke from nearby factories.

These steam-powered carriages are not merely a mode of transport; they are a symbol of the city's relentless progress and its embrace of technological innovation. They embody the spirit of an era where the boundaries of possibility are continually pushed, and every journey is a testament to the marvels of human ingenuity.

At the heart of the steam-powered carriages lies an intricate blend of raw steam power and precise clockwork mechanisms, a hallmark of Victorian engineering. The engine, a masterpiece of industrial design, is encased in a polished brass housing adorned with rivets and intricate engravings. Within, a boiler heated by coal or gas generates pressurized steam, the lifeblood of the vehicle, which is channeled through a series of valves and pistons.

The raw power of steam is harnessed by these pistons, which drive the carriages' wheels with formidable force. The pistons move with a rhythmic cadence, their polished surfaces gleaming as they convert thermal energy into mechanical motion. This powerful engine is capable of propelling the carriages at impressive speeds, ensuring swift and efficient transportation through the city's bustling streets.

Complementing this raw power is the precision of clockwork mechanisms, a delicate dance of gears, springs, and levers. These components, crafted with meticulous care, regulate the engine's operation, ensuring smooth and reliable performance. The clockwork gears, made of finely tempered steel and intricately interlocked, govern the timing of the pistons and the flow of steam, maintaining a harmonious balance between power and control.

A sophisticated network of linkages and cams translates the engine's linear motion into the rotational force needed to turn the wheels. These mechanisms are housed within beautifully crafted compartments, their movements visible through glass panels that allow onlookers to marvel at the precision engineering within. The interlocking gears and rotating shafts operate with a seamless elegance, a testament to the ingenuity of their designers.

The control system of the carriage is equally advanced, featuring brass-bound levers and dials that allow the driver to regulate speed and direction with ease. The levers connect to a series of rods and pulleys that transmit the driver's commands to the engine and steering mechanisms. Each component works in concert, ensuring that the vehicle responds instantly and accurately to the driver's inputs.

Safety features are also integrated into this advanced technology. Pressure gauges and safety valves monitor the steam levels, preventing overpressure and ensuring safe operation. The braking system, a marvel of mechanical engineering, utilizes both steam-powered and manual components to provide reliable stopping power, even under the most challenging conditions.

Together, the raw power of steam and the precision of clockwork mechanisms create a symphony of motion and control. This fusion of strength and finesse not only powers the carriages but also symbolizes the spirit of the age—a relentless pursuit of progress and perfection, where every journey is a testament to the wonders of Victorian innovation.

The streets are alive with activity, a vibrant tapestry of Victorian elegance and steampunk innovation. Crowds of people, dressed in period-appropriate attire, bustle about, their clothing reflecting the era's sophistication and the marvels of advanced technology.

Women in long dresses, their skirts adorned with layers of lace and satin, navigate the cobblestone streets with grace. Their ensembles are complemented by intricately designed corsets and high-collared blouses, often embellished with brass buttons and delicate embroidery. Many wear wide-brimmed hats adorned with feathers, ribbons, and mechanical accents, such as small gears or clockwork brooches, adding a touch of steampunk flair to their refined appearance.

Men, donning waistcoats and tailcoats, exude an air of distinguished elegance. Their outfits are completed with crisp white shirts, intricately knotted cravats, and brass cufflinks that catch the light with every movement. Top hats, polished to a gleaming finish, sit atop their heads, often adorned with goggles perched jauntily above the brim. These goggles, a fusion of fashion and function, feature brass frames and tinted lenses, essential for protecting their eyes from the soot and steam that permeate the city.

A quintessential steampunk accessory, goggles are worn not only by adventurers and engineers but also by fashionable city dwellers. These goggles come in various styles, from sleek brass frames with tinted glass lenses to more elaborate designs featuring multiple lenses and adjustable straps. They are often seen perched on hats, around necks, or even worn directly over the eyes.

Advanced technology has given rise to monocles that are more than mere eyewear. These monocles, crafted from chrome and brass, often include additional features such as magnification lenses, small dials for adjusting focus, and even tiny aetheric sensors that can detect minute changes in the environment. They are worn with pride, adding a touch of sophistication and scientific prowess to the wearer's ensemble.

Walking canes, more than just a symbol of status, are masterpieces of engineering. Fashioned from polished wood and reinforced with brass or chrome, these canes often conceal hidden gadgets. Some contain retractable telescopes, while others house miniature steam-powered mechanisms or secret compartments. The handles are intricately carved, sometimes featuring the likeness of mythical creatures or adorned with gemstones.

Brass pocket watches, hanging from intricately crafted chains, are a common sight, their ticking a constant reminder of the precise nature of time. Belts and sashes are adorned with small tools and gadgets, reflecting the practical aspect of steampunk fashion. Leather gloves, often reinforced with metal studs or intricate stitching, protect hands while adding a rugged touch to the attire.

The streets themselves mirror the fusion of the old and new. Cobblestone paths wind through the city, lined with ornate lampposts topped with gaslit globes. Market stalls and shopfronts display an array of goods, from freshly baked bread and exotic spices to mechanical trinkets and advanced aetheric devices.

Amidst the hustle and bustle, the air is filled with the sounds of steam-powered carriages clattering along, vendors calling out their wares, and the distant hum of dirigibles overhead. This vibrant scene, rich with the colors and textures of Victorian fashion and steampunk technology, paints a picture of a society at the height of its innovative and cultural prowess.

The streets are lined with various street vendors, their stalls brimming with newspapers, fresh fruits, and an assortment of other goods. The air is filled with the lively chatter of merchants calling out their wares and the hum of bustling activity. Shops with elaborate window displays showcase the latest fashions and technological innovations, drawing the attention of passersby.

Among the wares are clockwork devices, marvels of mechanical engineering that captivate onlookers with their intricate designs and precise movements. These devices range from pocket-sized automata that perform simple tasks, such as playing a tune or mimicking the chirp of a bird, to more complex contraptions like self-winding watches and miniature steam engines. The gears, cogs, and springs, often made of brass and silver, mesh together in perfect harmony, creating a mesmerizing display of mechanical prowess.

In the shop windows, one might also find automatons, life-sized mechanical beings crafted with astonishing detail and lifelike movements. These automatons serve various purposes, from performing household chores to entertaining guests with their graceful dances or playing musical instruments. Their exteriors are fashioned from polished metal and fine fabrics, and their eyes, made of glass or gemstone, gleam with an almost human intelligence. Each automaton is a testament to the ingenuity and artistry of its creator, blending function with aesthetic beauty.

At the forefront of the technological revolution are devices that harness the power of the hypersphere and electromagnetic technology. The hypersphere, a complex construct that transcends conventional three-dimensional space, is used to create advanced navigation tools and communication devices. These devices, with their sleek, metallic casings and glowing interfaces, allow for instantaneous travel and information exchange across vast distances, connecting different parts of the city and beyond with unprecedented efficiency.

The electromagnetic devices, on the other hand, utilize the principles of electromagnetism to power everything from streetlights to personal gadgets. These innovations include portable generators, magnetic locks, and even wireless transmitters that enable voice communication over long distances. The shop windows proudly display these cutting-edge technologies, each item representing a leap forward in the application of scientific principles.

At the heart of these advancements lies the concept of the Hyperverse, an interconnected realm where physical and digital realities merge. Devices designed to interact with the Hyperverse are prominently featured, their interfaces glowing with a soft, otherworldly light. These devices allow users to access a wealth of information, control machinery remotely, and even experience immersive virtual environments. The Hyperverse represents the pinnacle of human achievement, a limitless expanse where the boundaries of knowledge and imagination are constantly being pushed.

As the crowds move along the streets, they are drawn to these displays of innovation and craftsmanship. The vendors and shopkeepers, eager to share the wonders of the new age, engage with potential customers, demonstrating the functionality of their wares and extolling the virtues of the latest inventions. The atmosphere is one of excitement and possibility, where the blending of Victorian elegance and steampunk technology creates a vibrant and dynamic urban landscape.

The city was alive with a symphony of sounds that painted a vivid picture of its vibrant life and relentless energy. The constant clatter of hooves echoed through the cobblestone streets, a rhythmic backdrop to the hustle and bustle. Horse-drawn carriages and steam-powered vehicles moved in a seemingly choreographed dance, their wheels creating a continuous, comforting clatter.

The hiss of steam engines punctuated the air, releasing bursts of vapor that mingled with the early morning mist. These engines, driving everything from carriages to factory machinery, added a mechanical heartbeat to the city's soundtrack. The steady chugging and occasional whistle of steam trains in the distance provided a reminder of the industrial prowess that powered the metropolis.

Amidst this mechanical orchestra, the chatter of the crowd filled the air. People from all walks of life thronged the streets, their conversations creating a lively murmur. Voices overlapped as they discussed the latest news, bartered over goods, or exchanged pleasantries. Laughter, heated debates, and friendly greetings blended into a rich auditory tapestry that reflected the city's diverse and dynamic populace.

The occasional shout from street vendors rose above the din, their calls adding an energetic cadence to the ambient noise. "Fresh fruits, ripe and ready!" one vendor hollered, while another proclaimed, "Get your morning paper here, latest edition!" The vendors' cries were both a marketing tactic and a vital part of the city's daily rhythm, drawing customers to their stalls with persuasive enthusiasm.

Together, these sounds created an immersive experience, capturing the essence of a city where tradition and innovation coexisted in a harmonious blend. The constant clatter of hooves, the hiss of steam engines, the chatter of the crowd, and the occasional shout from street vendors formed a soundscape that was as much a part of the city's identity as its towering buildings and intricate technological marvels.

The city's vibrant atmosphere was a sensory feast, with a rich tapestry of smells that mingled in the air, painting an olfactory portrait of its diverse and bustling nature.

The smell of coal smoke was ever-present, a testament to the city's industrial heart. The scent, a blend of soot and sulfur, carried on the breeze from the numerous factories and steam engines that powered the metropolis. It was a sharp, acrid aroma that spoke of relentless progress and the constant hum of machinery.

Intertwined with this was the enticing aroma of fresh bread, wafting from nearby bakeries. The comforting scent of baked goods—crusty loaves, buttery pastries, and sweet rolls—provided a warm, inviting contrast to the harshness of the industrial fumes. It evoked images of bustling kitchens and bakers hard at work, their efforts offering a daily delight to the city's inhabitants.

Adding to this olfactory symphony was the distinct metallic scent of machinery, a sharp, clean smell that hinted at oil, grease, and polished metal. This scent was most noticeable near workshops and engineering hubs, where gears, pistons, and clockwork devices were crafted and maintained. It was the smell of innovation and meticulous craftsmanship, a reminder of the technological marvels that defined the era.

Together, these scents created a unique blend that was unmistakably the essence of the city. The mix of coal smoke, fresh bread from nearby bakeries, and the distinct metallic scent of machinery formed an olfactory landscape that was as integral to the city's identity as its sounds and sights. This aromatic blend told the story of a place where industry and everyday life intertwined, creating a dynamic and ever-evolving urban tapestry.

Dominating the skyline, several tall chimneys spewed steam and smoke, their presence a stark testament to the industrial revolution's profound impact on the city. These towering structures, constructed of red brick and reinforced with iron bands, rose above the rooftops, visible from almost every corner of the bustling metropolis.

Attached to factories and workshops scattered throughout the city, these chimneys were the lifeblood of industry, tirelessly venting the byproducts of relentless production. The smoke they emitted, a thick, dark plume, coiled upwards, blending into the hazy sky. This ever-present cloud of soot and vapor painted the air with shades of grey, a constant reminder of the city's ceaseless drive for progress and innovation.

The factories, with their immense brick facades and arched windows, hummed with activity. Inside, vast assembly lines and rows of steam-powered machines worked in unison, producing everything from textiles to intricate clockwork devices. The rhythmic chugging of pistons and the whir of gears echoed from within, mingling with the distant clang of metal and the hiss of escaping steam.

Workshops, smaller yet equally vital, were scattered throughout the city, their chimneys contributing to the collective exhalation of industry. These workshops were the creative hubs where inventors and craftsmen pushed the boundaries of technology, designing and fabricating the marvels that defined the steampunk era. The scent of hot metal and oil wafted from these establishments, adding to the city's rich olfactory tapestry.

As the day progressed, the shadows cast by these towering chimneys stretched across the cobblestone streets, their silhouettes a constant presence in the urban landscape. The city's inhabitants moved beneath them, going about their daily business.

Danny Martin wiped his hands on a grease-stained cloth, his face alight with the warm glow of the gas lamps flickering overhead. His workshop, a sprawling labyrinth of polished brass, gleaming steel, and countless clockwork mechanisms, hummed with life. The air was thick with the scent of oil and the faint tang of heated metal. A symphony of ticking, whirring, and the occasional hiss of steam filled the room, each sound a testament to Danny's tireless work and boundless creativity.

Against one wall stood a towering array of shelves, each crammed with meticulously organized tools, gears, and springs. Blueprints and sketches were pinned to the walls, depicting a myriad of fantastical inventions. A mechanical arm here, a self-winding chronometer there—each creation a marvel of engineering. Dominating the center of the room was Danny's latest project: a magnificent automaton, its intricately jointed limbs and finely detailed face showcasing the pinnacle of his craftsmanship.

Danny adjusted his goggles and leaned over the automaton, carefully tightening a bolt. The machine was nearly complete, its lifelike visage a blend of human and machine. Tiny, precise gears powered its movements, and delicate filigree adorned its surface, giving it an almost regal appearance. He stepped back, wiping a smudge of oil from his cheek, and admired his work. The automaton's eyes, made of polished glass, seemed to follow him around the room, a testament to the lifelike quality he had achieved.

"Perfect," Danny muttered to himself, a satisfied smile curling his lips. He turned to his workbench, where a small brass bird perched, its wings poised as if ready to take flight. With a deft twist of a key, the bird sprang to life, its wings flapping rhythmically, producing a melodic chiming sound. Danny chuckled, watching the bird hop along the bench, a whimsical contrast to the grandeur of his larger creations.

Just as Danny was about to return to his work on the automaton, the door to the workshop creaked open, and a familiar figure stepped inside. Professor Eleanor Langdon, a renowned expert in steam-powered technology and a frequent collaborator of Danny's, entered the room. Her sharp eyes scanned the workshop, taking in the organized chaos with a look of admiration.

"Busy as ever, I see," she remarked, her voice tinged with amusement. She approached Danny, her long coat sweeping the floor behind her.

"Eleanor!" Danny exclaimed, a genuine smile breaking across his face. "It's been too long. What brings you here today?"

Eleanor glanced at the automaton, her eyes widening slightly in appreciation. "I heard about your latest project and couldn't resist coming to see it for myself. You never cease to amaze me, Danny."

Danny chuckled, scratching the back of his head. "Well, it's still a work in progress, but it's coming along nicely. What do you think?"

Eleanor circled the automaton, her fingers lightly tracing the delicate engravings. "It's exquisite. The detail, the precision—it's like nothing I've ever seen before. You've outdone yourself."

"Thanks," Danny said, his cheeks flushing slightly at the praise. "I've been working on it day and night. But enough about my projects. How have you been? Any new developments in your research?"

Eleanor's eyes sparkled with excitement. "Actually, yes. I've been working on a new steam-powered propulsion system for airships. If it works as I hope, it could revolutionize air travel."

Danny's interest was piqued. "That sounds incredible. I'd love to hear more about it."

Eleanor nodded, launching into an enthusiastic explanation of her latest innovations. As she spoke, Danny couldn't help but marvel at her brilliance. They had always shared a mutual passion for pushing the boundaries of technology, and their collaborations had led to some of their most groundbreaking inventions.

As they discussed their projects, the door to the workshop opened once again, and Dr. Victor Hargrove entered, his tall frame casting a shadow across the room. He was a distinguished figure in the field of steam technology, known for his work on automata and mechanical prosthetics. His presence added an air of gravity to the already charged atmosphere.

"Ah, I see I'm not the only one drawn to the allure of Danny's workshop," Victor said with a smile, his deep voice resonating in the space. He approached the automaton, his keen eyes inspecting its intricate details.

"Victor, welcome," Danny greeted, shaking his hand. "It's good to see you."

Victor nodded, his gaze still fixed on the automaton. "This is truly remarkable, Danny. You've surpassed even my high expectations. The craftsmanship, the complexity—it's a masterpiece."

Danny felt a swell of pride at the compliment. "Thank you, Victor. I've poured my heart and soul into this one."

Victor turned his attention to Eleanor. "And what about you, Eleanor? Any new breakthroughs in your work?"

Eleanor smiled, her excitement evident. "I'm working on a steam-powered propulsion system for airships. If it succeeds, it could change the way we travel."

Victor raised an eyebrow, clearly intrigued. "That sounds like a game-changer. I'd love to see it in action."

As the three of them continued to discuss their respective projects, the workshop seemed to hum with even more energy. Ideas flowed freely, and the air was thick with the promise of innovation and discovery. Danny, Eleanor, and Victor had always found inspiration in each other's work, and their collaborative efforts had led to some of the most significant advancements in steam technology.

Their conversation was interrupted by a soft chime from the corner of the room. Danny glanced over and saw Miss Arabella Fairchild, his trusted assistant, entering the workshop. She was a young woman with a keen intellect and a knack for solving complex problems. Her presence always brought a sense of order and efficiency to the workshop.

"Excuse me, Danny," Arabella said, her voice calm and measured. "I've finished calibrating the steam engines for the new airship model. Would you like to inspect them?"

Danny nodded, appreciative of her diligence. "Of course, Arabella. Lead the way."

He turned to Eleanor and Victor. "Please, make yourselves at home. I'll be back shortly."

Arabella led Danny to a smaller section of the workshop, where a series of miniature steam engines were arranged in a precise row. Each engine was a marvel of engineering, its polished brass components gleaming under the workshop lights. Danny inspected them closely, noting the meticulous attention to detail in their construction.

"Excellent work, Arabella," he said, nodding approvingly. "These engines are perfect. They should provide the power we need for the airship."

Arabella smiled, a hint of pride in her eyes. "Thank you, Danny. I'm glad you're pleased with them."

As they returned to the main workshop, Danny couldn't help but feel a sense of satisfaction. Surrounded by his creations and his colleagues, he knew they were on the cusp of something truly extraordinary. The future of steam technology was bright, and together, they would continue to push the boundaries of what was possible.

Back in the workshop, Eleanor and Victor were deep in conversation, their animated gestures highlighting their passion for their work. Danny joined them, eager to hear more about their latest ideas.

"Eleanor was just telling me about her propulsion system," Victor said, his eyes alight with excitement. "It's revolutionary. The potential applications are endless."

Eleanor nodded, her enthusiasm palpable. "I've been working on a prototype, and I think it could change the way we think about air travel. Imagine airships that can travel faster and more efficiently than ever before."

Danny's mind raced with possibilities. "We could combine our efforts. With your propulsion system, Eleanor, and our advancements in automation, we could create airships that are not only faster but also more capable than anything currently in existence."

Victor's eyes gleamed with anticipation. "And with the precision of Danny's automata, we could automate many of the ship's functions, making air travel safer and more reliable."

The three of them continued to brainstorm, their ideas flowing freely and building upon each other. The workshop, already a hub of innovation, seemed to pulse with a renewed sense of purpose. They knew they were on the brink of something extraordinary, a breakthrough that could reshape the future of steam technology.

As the evening wore on, the gas lamps cast long shadows across the room, and the hum of machinery became a soothing backdrop to their discussion. The possibilities were endless, and the excitement of discovery spurred them on. In that moment, surrounded by their inventions and fueled by their shared passion, they felt invincible.

Danny looked around at his workshop, at the intricate machines and the brilliant minds gathered there, and felt a profound sense of gratitude. They were more than colleagues; they were pioneers, explorers in the vast and uncharted territory of steam technology. And together, they would forge a path to a future filled with wonder and possibility.

As the night deepened and the first light of dawn began to creep through the workshop windows, the trio continued to talk, plan, and dream.

Chapter Two: The Mysterious Letter

As the first light of dawn filtered through the workshop windows, casting a warm glow on the brass and steel surfaces, a sharp rap at the door interrupted their discussion. Danny looked up, surprised. It was unusual for visitors to come by so early.

"Who could that be at this hour?" he muttered, wiping his hands on a rag as he walked to the door. Eleanor and Victor exchanged curious glances, pausing their animated conversation.

Danny opened the door to find a small, bespectacled boy standing there, holding a slightly crumpled envelope. The boy looked up at him with wide eyes, his clothes indicating he was likely a messenger from the nearby post office.

"Good morning, sir. A letter for you," the boy said, handing the envelope to Danny.

"Thank you," Danny replied, giving the boy a coin for his trouble. The boy tipped his cap and scurried off, disappearing down the cobbled street.

Danny closed the door and examined the envelope. It was made of thick, yellowed parchment, and his name was written in an elegant, flowing script. There was no return address, only an intricate wax seal bearing an unfamiliar crest.

"Interesting," Danny mused, breaking the seal and unfolding the letter. Eleanor and Victor watched with growing curiosity as he read the contents.

Danny's eyes widened as he scanned the letter. It was written in the same elegant script as the address, but the message was cryptic:

"To Danny Martin,

Your talents are known far and wide, and it is for this reason that I seek your help. Strange occurrences have been reported in the outskirts of the city, all linked to an ancient steam engine believed to possess extraordinary powers.

If you value the progress of our beloved steam technology, meet me at midnight by the old clock tower.

Yours in secrecy,

A Friend"

Danny looked up from the letter, his mind racing. "It seems we have a mystery on our hands," he said, handing the letter to Eleanor.

She read it quickly, her brow furrowing. "An ancient steam engine with extraordinary powers? This sounds like something out of a legend."

Victor took the letter next, his eyes narrowing in thought. "Whoever wrote this knows of your reputation, Danny. And the fact that they chose to remain anonymous suggests that this matter is both urgent and sensitive."

Danny nodded, his excitement growing. "There's only one way to find out. We must go to the old clock tower at midnight."

Eleanor and Victor exchanged a glance, both intrigued and concerned. "We should be cautious," Eleanor advised. "This could be a trap, or at the very least, something far more dangerous than we realize."

"Agreed," Victor added. "But if there's even a chance that this steam engine exists and possesses such powers, we cannot ignore it."

Danny looked at his friends, their determination mirroring his own. "Then it's settled. We'll meet at the clock tower tonight."

The day passed in a blur of preparations. Danny double-checked his tools and made sure his mechanical bird was in working order. Eleanor gathered her notes and brought along a portable steam analyzer. Victor, ever the cautious one, prepared a small arsenal of defensive gadgets, just in case.

As night fell and the city streets grew quiet, the three of them set out for the old clock tower. The structure loomed in the distance, its silhouette stark against the moonlit sky. The clock, long since stopped, stood as a silent sentinel over the deserted square.

They arrived just before midnight, the air crisp and cool. Danny glanced around, his senses alert for any sign of movement. The letter had mentioned strange occurrences, and he was prepared for anything.

A shadow detached itself from the darkness, and a figure stepped forward, cloaked in a heavy, hooded coat. The figure's face was obscured, but a glint of light reflected off the lenses of their goggles.

"Thank you for coming," the figure said, their voice low and calm. "I was not sure you would."

"We're here," Danny replied, trying to sound confident. "Who are you, and what do you know about this steam engine?"

The figure pulled back their hood, revealing the face of an older man, his features lined with age and worry. His eyes, however, were sharp and intelligent. "My name is Archibald Graves. I am a historian and an expert on ancient steam technology. What I am about to tell you may sound unbelievable, but I assure you, it is the truth."

Archibald reached into his coat and pulled out a small, intricately detailed brass device. "This," he said, holding it up for them to see, "is a fragment of the engine I mentioned. It is unlike anything I have ever encountered."

Eleanor stepped closer, examining the fragment with keen interest. "Remarkable. The craftsmanship is exquisite. But what makes you think it has extraordinary powers?"

Archibald's expression grew grave. "This fragment was recovered from the site of a recent incident. A small village on the outskirts of the city experienced a series of inexplicable events—lights flickering without any apparent source, machinery coming to life on its own, and strange, almost ghostly figures appearing in the night. All of these occurrences began after an excavation uncovered the remains of an ancient steam engine."

Victor frowned. "And you believe this engine is responsible?"

Archibald nodded. "I do. The engine is unlike anything recorded in our history. It predates our current understanding of steam technology, and yet, it is far more advanced. I believe it harnesses a form of energy we have yet to comprehend."

Danny felt a chill run down his spine. The implications of such a discovery were staggering. "Where is this engine now?"

Archibald hesitated. "It is still in the village, hidden away to prevent further disturbances. I came to you because I need your expertise to understand and possibly contain it. If we can unlock its secrets, it could change the future of steam technology forever."

Eleanor looked at Danny, her eyes alight with determination. "We have to see it for ourselves. If there's even a chance that this engine is real, we can't ignore it."

Victor nodded in agreement. "But we must proceed with caution. We don't know what we're dealing with."

Danny turned to Archibald. "Lead the way. We'll help you, but we need to see this engine and understand what we're facing."

Archibald nodded, relief evident on his face. "Thank you. Follow me, and I'll take you to the village. It's a bit of a journey, but I believe you will find it worth the effort."

As they set off into the night, Danny couldn't shake the feeling that they were on the brink of a discovery that could redefine everything they knew about steam technology. The ancient engine held secrets that had been buried for centuries, and he was determined to uncover them.

The journey to the village was long and arduous, but the anticipation kept them moving. As dawn began to break, they arrived at the outskirts of the small, isolated village. The air was thick with an eerie stillness, and the villagers they passed cast wary glances at the newcomers.

Archibald led them to a modest house on the edge of the village, where he had been staying. Inside, the air was filled with the faint scent of aged wood and the quiet ticking of a grandfather clock. He gestured for them to sit around a large wooden table, spreading out a detailed map of the village and the excavation site.

"This is where we found the engine," Archibald explained, pointing to a location marked with an 'X' on the map. "It's hidden in an underground chamber, protected by layers of earth and stone. We need to be careful not to disturb the balance, as the engine seems to react to changes in its environment."

Danny studied the map, his mind racing with possibilities. "We'll need to document everything and proceed methodically. Eleanor, can you set up the steam analyzer? We'll need to take readings as we go."

Eleanor nodded, already unpacking her equipment. "Of course. We need to understand the energy this engine is producing and how it's affecting the surroundings."

Victor, ever the pragmatist, began to check his defensive gadgets. "I'll keep watch and make sure we're not disturbed. If there are any strange occurrences, we need to be ready."

With their plan in place, the group set out for the excavation site. The village was still shrouded in a heavy silence, and the early morning mist added an ethereal quality to their surroundings. Danny's heart pounded with a mix of excitement and trepidation. They were about to uncover a piece of history that could change everything.

Chapter Three: First Encounter

As they made their way to the excavation site, the morning mist began to lift, revealing the quaint, cobblestone streets of the village. The houses, with their steeply pitched roofs and smoke curling from chimneys, exuded an air of rustic charm. Despite this, an undercurrent of unease permeated the air, as if the village itself was holding its breath.

At the excavation site, they found a gaping hole in the ground, surrounded by piles of earth and stone. The remnants of old machinery lay scattered around, hinting at the age of the steam engine buried below. Danny and Eleanor set up the steam analyzer, while Victor stood guard, his eyes scanning the horizon for any signs of disturbance.

"Here it is," Archibald said, leading them to the entrance of the underground chamber. "The engine is just beyond this passage."

Danny nodded, gripping his tools tightly. "Let's proceed carefully. We don't know what kind of mechanisms might be in place."

They descended into the dark, narrow passage, their lanterns casting flickering shadows on the stone walls. The air grew colder as they ventured deeper, and the faint hum of machinery grew louder, echoing through the corridor.

Finally, they entered a large underground chamber, the centerpiece of which was the ancient steam engine. It was an impressive sight, its brass and steel components intricately intertwined, covered in a patina of age. The engine seemed almost alive, its gears turning slowly, emitting a faint, rhythmic pulse.

Eleanor immediately set to work with the steam analyzer, taking readings and muttering to herself as she interpreted the data. "This is extraordinary," she said, her voice tinged with awe. "The energy readings are off the charts. This engine is harnessing a power source we've never seen before."

Danny approached the engine, his eyes scanning its surface for any clues. "We need to understand how it works and what it's connected to. If this engine is affecting the village, it could have far-reaching consequences."

As they studied the engine, a sudden jolt shook the chamber, and the lights flickered. Danny's heart raced. "What was that?"

Victor, who had been keeping watch, moved closer to the group. "It came from above. We need to check the village."

They hurried back to the surface, where they found the villagers gathered in the square, their faces filled with fear and confusion. The power grid had malfunctioned, plunging parts of the village into darkness.

Danny and his team quickly assessed the situation. "We need to find the source of the malfunction," Danny said, his mind racing with possibilities. "It could be connected to the steam engine."

They followed the power lines to a central hub near the village center. The machinery there was old but well-maintained, a testament to the villagers' resourcefulness. However, it was clear that something had gone wrong.

Eleanor examined the control panel, her brow furrowed in concentration. "There's a massive power surge coming from somewhere. It's overloading the system."

Danny scanned the area, his eyes landing on a series of cables leading back to the excavation site. "The engine. It must be connected to the grid somehow."

Victor nodded. "That would explain the sudden malfunction. If the engine is generating more power than the grid can handle, it could cause a surge like this."

Archibald, who had been listening intently, spoke up. "The engine was likely built to harness and distribute energy. If we can understand its mechanisms, we might be able to control it."

With a sense of urgency, they returned to the underground chamber. Danny approached the engine, examining its connections more closely. "There must be a way to regulate the power output," he said, his mind working through the possibilities.

Eleanor continued to take readings, her fingers flying over the controls of the steam analyzer. "The energy patterns are consistent with a type of harmonic resonance. If we can find the right frequency, we might be able to stabilize the output."

Victor stood guard, his eyes and ears alert for any signs of danger. "We need to hurry. Another surge could cause serious damage."

Danny nodded, focusing intently on the engine. He adjusted a series of dials and levers, trying to find the right configuration. The engine responded, its hum growing steadier, the pulse of its gears more rhythmic.

"Almost there," Danny muttered, making a final adjustment. The engine's hum stabilized, and the lights in the chamber grew brighter.

Eleanor checked the readings. "The output is stabilizing. We did it."

Relief washed over them as they realized they had averted a potential disaster. However, Danny knew their work was far from over. "We need to find a permanent solution. This engine holds incredible power, but we need to understand it fully to use it safely."

As they emerged from the underground chamber, the villagers greeted them with a mix of curiosity and gratitude. Danny addressed the crowd, explaining what they had discovered and reassuring them that they were working to ensure their safety.

Over the next few days, Danny and his team worked tirelessly to understand the ancient steam engine. They pored over the blueprints, consulted with experts, and experimented with different configurations. Slowly but surely, they began to unravel the engine's secrets.

Eleanor discovered that the engine used a form of crystal lattice to generate and store energy, a technology far more advanced than anything they had seen before. Victor identified a series of safety mechanisms built into the engine, designed to prevent overloads and ensure stable operation.

Danny, with his knack for mechanical systems, devised a way to integrate the engine with the village's power grid, using a series of regulators and converters to manage the flow of energy. It was a complex and delicate process, but with each step, they grew more confident.

One evening, as they were putting the final touches on the system, a loud knock echoed through the workshop. Danny opened the door to find a group of government officials standing outside, their expressions serious.

"We've heard about your discoveries," the leader said, stepping forward. "The implications of this ancient engine are immense. We need to ensure it is used responsibly and doesn't fall into the wrong hands."

Danny felt a mix of pride and apprehension. "We're doing everything we can to understand and control it. But you're right, this technology must be handled with care."

The officials inspected the setup, asking detailed questions and taking notes. They were impressed by the team's progress and agreed to provide additional resources to ensure the engine's safe integration with the village's power grid.

In the days that followed, the village became a hub of activity. Engineers, scientists, and scholars arrived to study the ancient engine, drawn by the promise of unlocking its secrets. Danny, Eleanor, and Victor found themselves at the center of a whirlwind of innovation and discovery.

Through it all, Danny remained focused on the task at hand. The engine was a marvel of engineering, but it was also a responsibility. He knew that with great power came great potential for both progress and peril.

As the village's power grid stabilized and the mysterious occurrences ceased, Danny allowed himself a moment of reflection. They had come a long way from the quiet days in his workshop, surrounded by his inventions. The ancient steam engine had opened a new chapter in their lives, filled with possibilities and challenges.

One evening, as the sun set and the village settled into a peaceful rhythm, Danny stood by the ancient steam engine, now fully integrated and stable. He thought about the journey they had taken, the mysteries they had unraveled, and the future that lay ahead.

Eleanor joined him, her eyes reflecting the soft glow of the engine. "We've come a long way, haven't we?"

Danny nodded, a smile playing on his lips. "Yes, we have. And this is just the beginning. There's so much more to discover."

Victor approached, his usually serious expression softened by a rare smile. "To think, it all started with a mysterious letter. Who knows what other secrets are out there, waiting to be uncovered?"

Danny looked at his friends, his heart swelling with gratitude and determination. "Whatever the future holds, we'll face it together. We've proven that when we combine our talents and our passions, we can achieve the extraordinary."

As the stars began to twinkle in the night sky, Danny, Eleanor, and Victor stood together, ready to embrace the challenges and opportunities that lay ahead.

Chapter Four: The Strange Occurrence

The tranquility of the village was shattered one fateful night by a thunderous explosion that echoed through the streets, shaking buildings and sending a plume of steam and smoke into the sky. The sound was deafening, and the shockwave knocked people off their feet. Lights flickered and went out, and the hum of machinery abruptly ceased, plunging the village into an eerie silence.

Danny, Eleanor, and Victor were jolted awake by the blast. They rushed to the source of the explosion, their hearts pounding with fear and adrenaline. As they approached the village square, they were met with a scene of chaos. Debris was scattered everywhere, and villagers were running in all directions, their faces etched with panic.

"The power grid!" Danny shouted over the din, pointing to the central hub. It was the epicenter of the explosion, now a smoking ruin. Sparks flew from damaged wires, and the air was thick with the acrid smell of burnt metal.

"We need to get this under control!" Eleanor yelled, already heading towards the control panel. "Victor, can you help contain the damage?"

Victor nodded, his face set with determination. "I'll do my best. Danny, see if you can find out what caused this."

Danny nodded, his mind racing. He knew the power grid had been stable before the explosion, and the sudden malfunction seemed too coincidental. As he navigated through the chaos, he couldn't shake the feeling that something sinister was at play.

He reached the remains of the power grid and began examining the wreckage. His sharp eyes quickly picked out anomalies—wires that had been deliberately cut, components that had been tampered with. It was clear that this was no accident.

"Someone did this on purpose," he muttered to himself, his anger rising. "But who? And why?"

As he continued his investigation, he noticed a faint trail of footprints leading away from the scene. They were almost invisible in the dim light, but Danny's keen eyes caught the slight disturbances in the dust and debris. He followed the trail, his mind focused and his senses alert.

The footprints led him to a secluded part of the village, where an old, abandoned warehouse stood. The building was dark and silent, but Danny could sense movement inside. He approached cautiously, peering through a broken window.

Inside, he saw a group of figures huddled around a strange device. It was a smaller version of the ancient steam engine, but it was modified in ways that made it look even more dangerous. The figures were busy adjusting dials and levers, their faces obscured by hoods.

Danny's heart raced as he realized the implications. These people had deliberately sabotaged the power grid to create chaos, and now they were working on something even more destructive.

He crept around to the back of the warehouse, searching for a way in. He found a small door and carefully eased it open, slipping inside without making a sound. As he moved closer to the group, he could hear snippets of their conversation.

"...need to hurry. The explosion was just the beginning. Once this device is activated, it will cripple the entire city's infrastructure."

Danny's blood ran cold. He had to stop them before they could carry out their plan. He scanned the room, looking for something he could use as a weapon. His eyes landed on a heavy wrench lying on a nearby workbench. He grabbed it, feeling its weight in his hand.

Taking a deep breath, he stepped out from the shadows. "Stop right there!"

The figures turned in surprise, their hoods falling back to reveal their faces. Danny recognized one of them immediately—it was Maxwell, a former colleague who had been expelled from their circle for unethical experiments.

"Danny Martin," Maxwell sneered, his eyes gleaming with malice. "I should have known you'd stick your nose where it doesn't belong."

"You've gone too far this time, Maxwell," Danny replied, tightening his grip on the wrench. "This ends now."

Maxwell laughed, a cold, cruel sound. "You're too late, Danny. The device is already primed. In a matter of minutes, it will unleash a wave of steam that will bring the entire city to its knees."

Danny's mind raced as he tried to think of a way to stop the device. He couldn't let Maxwell succeed. He lunged forward, swinging the wrench at the device. Maxwell's accomplices moved to intercept him, but Danny's determination gave him strength. He fought them off, his every move fueled by the urgency of the situation.

Finally, he reached the device and brought the wrench down on its control panel, smashing it with all his might. Sparks flew, and the device emitted a high-pitched whine as it began to power down.

Maxwell roared in anger and lunged at Danny, but Danny was ready. He sidestepped the attack and struck Maxwell with the wrench, knocking him to the ground. The other accomplices, seeing their leader defeated, fled into the night.

Breathing heavily, Danny inspected the damaged device. It was no longer a threat, but the village was still in chaos. He needed to get back and help restore order.

He hurried back to the village square, where Eleanor and Victor were still working tirelessly to stabilize the power grid. "I found the saboteurs," he said, his voice strained but triumphant. "They were planning something much worse, but I managed to stop them."

Eleanor looked up, relief and gratitude in her eyes. "Thank goodness. But we still need to repair the damage here."

Victor nodded. "We'll get it done. With your help, Danny, we can make sure this never happens again."

As they worked together to restore the power grid, Danny couldn't help but think about the challenges they had faced and the ones still to come. The ancient steam engine had brought them together, but it had also attracted danger. They would need to be vigilant and prepared for whatever came next.

By dawn, the power grid was stable once more, and the villagers were beginning to calm down. Danny, Eleanor, and Victor stood together, exhausted but resolute.

"We've made it through this crisis," Danny said, his voice filled with determination. "But we can't let our guard down. Maxwell and his kind are still out there, and they'll stop at nothing to harness the power of the ancient steam engine."

Eleanor nodded. "We'll continue our work, improving and protecting the technology we've discovered. And we'll be ready for whatever comes next."

Victor placed a hand on Danny's shoulder. "Together, we can face any challenge. We've proven that tonight."

As the first light of dawn bathed the village in a soft, golden glow, Danny felt a renewed sense of purpose. They had overcome a great danger, but their journey was far from over. The future was uncertain, but with friends like Eleanor and Victor by his side, he knew they could face it head-on.

And so, with the village beginning to stir back to life, Danny, Eleanor, and Victor set out to continue their work, ready to uncover more mysteries and protect the incredible power they had discovered. The ancient steam engine was both a marvel and a menace, and they would do everything in their power to ensure it was used for the greater good.

Chapter Five: Gathering Clues

As the sun rose higher, casting long shadows across the village, Danny, Eleanor, and Victor decided it was time to delve deeper into the mystery surrounding the ancient steam engine. They had thwarted Maxwell's immediate plans, but the incident had made it clear that their work was far from over.

Back in Danny's workshop, the trio sat around a large oak table cluttered with tools, papers, and artifacts. Danny unrolled the blueprint he had retrieved from the underground chamber, spreading it out carefully. The intricate lines and symbols were both mesmerizing and perplexing.

"I've never seen anything like this," Eleanor said, her eyes scanning the detailed schematics. "These designs are far more advanced than anything we've developed. It's like looking into the future."

Victor nodded, his gaze intense. "We need to understand every aspect of this engine. If Maxwell could figure out how to misuse its power, others could too."

Danny's thoughts drifted back to the cryptic letter that had set them on this path. He wondered if there were more clues hidden in the village, or perhaps in places they had yet to explore. Determined to leave no stone unturned, he suggested they revisit the excavation site to search for any overlooked documents or artifacts.

The excavation site was still in disarray from the recent turmoil. As they carefully sifted through the rubble, Eleanor uncovered a hidden compartment in one of the walls. Inside, they found a dusty leather-bound journal and several aged blueprints.

"This looks promising," she said, handing the journal to Danny.

Danny opened the journal, his eyes widening as he read the first entry. It was written in a neat, precise hand, dated over a century ago. The author was none other than his great-grandfather, William Martin, a renowned inventor of his time.

"These are my great-grandfather's writings," Danny said, his voice filled with awe. "He was involved with the creation of this engine."

He turned the pages carefully, absorbing the detailed accounts of experiments, discoveries, and the development of the steam engine. William Martin had been a visionary, his work driven by a deep curiosity and a relentless pursuit of knowledge. But as Danny read on, he found entries that hinted at something more ominous.

"June 12, 1879: The engine's capabilities far exceed my initial expectations. It appears to tap into a form of energy I cannot fully comprehend. The power it generates is both awe-inspiring and terrifying. I must proceed with caution."

"July 8, 1880: Strange phenomena have begun to occur. Machinery operating without any visible source of power, lights flickering in the dead of night. I fear the engine may be responsible, but I cannot yet determine how."

"August 14, 1881: I have discovered a connection between the engine and a series of ancient texts. They speak of an artifact that can control this energy, a key of sorts. I must find it before the engine's power becomes uncontrollable."

As Danny read these entries aloud, Eleanor and Victor exchanged worried glances. The journal confirmed their suspicions—the engine was capable of extraordinary, and potentially dangerous, feats.

"We need to find this artifact," Victor said, his voice resolute. "If it can control the engine's power, it's crucial to our understanding and safety."

Eleanor examined the blueprints they had found alongside the journal. "These schematics show modifications that William made to the engine. He must have been trying to harness or limit its power."

Danny nodded, his mind racing with possibilities. "My great-grandfather left these clues for a reason. He wanted us to continue his work and find a way to safely manage the engine's power."

With renewed determination, the trio returned to the workshop to study the blueprints and journal in greater detail. Danny carefully traced the lines of the schematics, trying to decipher his great-grandfather's intentions.

Eleanor, meanwhile, poured over the journal, searching for any mention of the artifact. "There's a passage here," she said, pointing to a section of the text. "William mentions a hidden compartment within the engine itself, where he stored something important. It could be the artifact."

Excitement buzzed in the air as they realized they might be on the verge of a significant breakthrough. They decided to investigate the hidden compartment immediately.

Back at the underground chamber, Danny approached the ancient steam engine with a mixture of reverence and anticipation. He ran his hands over its surface, searching for any signs of a hidden mechanism. After several minutes, he found a small, almost imperceptible latch. With a steady hand, he pressed it, and a concealed panel slid open, revealing a small metal box.

Inside the box was an intricately designed key, made of a strange, shimmering metal. Alongside it was a note in William's handwriting.

"To whomever finds this: This key is the artifact I have sought. It is the only means to control the engine's immense power. Use it wisely, and guard it well. The future depends on it."

Danny held the key up, the weight of his great-grandfather's legacy pressing heavily on his shoulders. "We've found it," he said softly. "This is the key to controlling the engine."

Eleanor and Victor leaned in, examining the key with fascination. "It's beautiful," Eleanor said, tracing the intricate patterns etched into the metal. "But how does it work?"

"We need to study it further," Danny replied. "And we must ensure it's kept safe from anyone who might misuse it."

With the key and the journal in hand, they returned to the workshop to begin their analysis. Days turned into nights as they pored over the documents, experimenting with the key and the engine, trying to unlock its secrets.

One evening, as they were deep in their research, a knock at the door startled them. Danny opened it to find an elderly man standing there, his eyes sharp and penetrating.

"Good evening," the man said, his voice smooth and authoritative. "My name is Reginald Hawthorne. I'm a historian with a particular interest in ancient steam technology. I've heard about your discoveries and would like to offer my assistance."

Danny hesitated, glancing back at Eleanor and Victor. They had been cautious about who they shared their findings with, but Hawthorne's knowledge could prove invaluable.

"Please, come in," Danny said, stepping aside. "We could use all the help we can get."

Hawthorne entered the workshop, his eyes immediately drawn to the blueprints and the journal spread out on the table. "Remarkable," he said, examining the documents. "William Martin was a genius ahead of his time. I've studied his work extensively, but these writings reveal even more than I imagined."

As they shared their findings with Hawthorne, his insights proved invaluable. He identified references in the journal that they had overlooked and suggested new avenues of research. With his help, they made significant progress in understanding the engine's capabilities and the key's role in controlling it.

However, as their understanding grew, so did the dangers. Word of their discoveries spread, and soon, they were facing increased scrutiny from both allies and adversaries. Maxwell, though thwarted, was still at large, and other factions were becoming interested in the ancient steam engine and its potential power.

One night, as they were deep in discussion, the workshop door burst open, and a group of armed men stormed in. At their head was Maxwell, his face twisted with fury and determination.

"You thought you could stop me, Danny," Maxwell snarled. "But you only delayed the inevitable. That engine's power belongs to me, and I will have it."

Danny stood his ground, the key hidden securely in his pocket. "You'll never get your hands on it, Maxwell. This power is too dangerous to be controlled by someone like you."

Maxwell's eyes gleamed with malice. "We'll see about that. Seize them!"

A fierce struggle ensued as Danny, Eleanor, Victor, and Hawthorne fought to protect their work and the key. The air was filled with the sounds of clashing metal and the hiss of steam as they defended themselves against Maxwell's men.

In the chaos, Danny managed to activate a defensive mechanism built into the workshop. Gears whirred to life, and steam-powered traps ensnared several of Maxwell's men, but the battle was far from over.

Eleanor and Victor fought side by side, their skills complementing each other perfectly. Hawthorne, despite his age, proved to be a formidable ally, his knowledge of steam technology giving them a crucial edge.

Amid the struggle, Danny found himself face to face with Maxwell. The two men circled each other, the tension palpable.

"You can't win, Maxwell," Danny said, his voice steady. "This engine's power is beyond your control."

Maxwell sneered. "I don't need to control it, Danny. I just need to possess it. And I'll destroy anyone who stands in my way."

The two clashed, the fight intense and brutal. Danny used every ounce of his strength and ingenuity, but Maxwell was relentless. As the battle raged, Danny caught a glimpse of the key, its metal gleaming in the dim light.

With a surge of determination, he reached for the key, feeling its power in his grasp. Using it, he managed to tap into the engine's energy, channeling it in a focused burst that knocked Maxwell off his feet.

Maxwell's men, seeing their leader defeated, retreated, leaving the workshop in disarray. Panting and battered, Danny stood over Maxwell, who lay unconscious on the floor.

Eleanor, Victor, and Hawthorne gathered around, their faces a mix of relief and concern. "We need to secure the engine and the key," Eleanor said urgently. "This isn't over yet."

Danny nodded, his resolve stronger than ever. "We'll protect this technology, and we'll make sure it's used for the greater good. We need to lock everything down and ensure no one else can exploit it."

With Maxwell defeated and his men scattered, the immediate threat had passed, but the team knew that they were far from safe. They worked tirelessly through the night, reinforcing the workshop's defenses and securing the ancient steam engine. Hawthorne's expertise proved invaluable in designing new protective measures that integrated seamlessly with Danny's existing systems.

The next morning, as the sun's first rays illuminated the village, a sense of uneasy calm settled over the area. The villagers, though shaken by the recent events, began to return to their daily routines, reassured by the presence of Danny and his team.

Danny, Eleanor, Victor, and Hawthorne gathered around the workshop table, the blueprints and journal spread before them. The key lay in the center, its shimmering metal catching the light.

"We've made significant progress," Hawthorne said, his voice steady but tinged with urgency. "But we must uncover the full extent of this engine's capabilities and its connection to your family, Danny. There may be more hidden dangers or opportunities that we've yet to discover."

Danny nodded, his eyes fixed on the key. "My great-grandfather left these clues for a reason. He must have known that this technology would resurface one day. We need to follow his trail and find any other hidden insights or safeguards he might have put in place."

Eleanor traced her finger over the journal's pages. "There's a passage here that mentions a secondary location—an old laboratory on the outskirts of the city. William writes about storing additional research and prototypes there."

Victor looked up, his expression resolute. "Then that's our next destination. We need to secure any remaining information and technology before it falls into the wrong hands."

With their plan set, they prepared to leave for the old laboratory. They traveled by steam carriage, the journey taking them through the winding streets and into the more isolated parts of the city. The laboratory, they discovered, was hidden within a dense grove of trees, its entrance cleverly concealed by foliage and overgrowth.

The building itself was a marvel of Victorian architecture, its brick walls and wrought iron details giving it an air of forgotten grandeur. Danny led the way, his heart pounding with anticipation. They forced open the rusted doors, revealing a dimly lit interior filled with dust-covered machinery and shelves lined with books and papers.

Eleanor and Victor began cataloging the contents, while Danny and Hawthorne focused on a large, ornately decorated safe at the back of the room. It was protected by a complex mechanical lock, one that only someone with Danny's skills could decipher.

Danny worked meticulously, his fingers deftly manipulating the intricate mechanisms. After several tense moments, there was a satisfying click, and the safe door swung open. Inside, they found a trove of blueprints, diagrams, and another journal, this one even older than the first.

Hawthorne's eyes widened as he scanned the documents. "These are incredible. Your great-grandfather was working on technologies far ahead of his time. And this journal—it belongs to his mentor, Dr. Elias Hargrove."

Danny opened the ancient journal, its pages filled with neat, precise writing and detailed sketches. Dr. Hargrove's entries provided a deeper understanding of the steam engine's origins and its potential.

"November 22, 1870: The engine's power is derived from a rare mineral found deep within the earth. This mineral, when properly harnessed, can generate immense energy, far beyond our current capabilities. But its use comes with great risk."

"December 15, 1871: I have constructed a series of prototypes to better understand the mineral's properties. Each prototype reveals new facets of its potential, but also new dangers. I must proceed with caution."

"January 3, 1872: William and I have devised a key to control the engine's power, a safeguard against its misuse. This key must be kept secret and protected at all costs."

As Danny read these passages aloud, a sense of clarity and purpose settled over him. His great-grandfather and Dr. Hargrove had laid the groundwork for understanding and controlling the engine's power. It was now up to him and his team to complete their work.

"We need to secure this mineral," Eleanor said, her mind already working through the possibilities. "If we can understand its properties, we might be able to create a sustainable and controlled source of energy."

Victor nodded. "And we need to continue refining the key's design. The more control we have, the safer we can make this technology."

Hawthorne, ever the historian, added, "We should also consider the implications of our discoveries. This mineral and the engine's power could revolutionize our world, but we must ensure it's used responsibly."

With their newfound knowledge, Danny and his team returned to the workshop, their determination stronger than ever. They spent days and nights immersed in their work, drawing on the wisdom of the past to forge a path forward.

As they refined their designs and conducted experiments, they made remarkable progress. The key's design was improved, providing even greater control over the engine's power. They also developed new safety mechanisms to prevent any future tampering or sabotage.

Eleanor's research into the mineral led to the discovery of a small deposit within the city. With careful extraction and testing, they confirmed its potential as a powerful and sustainable energy source. However, they also realized that its rarity meant it had to be used judiciously.

Despite their successes, the threat of Maxwell and others like him loomed large. Danny knew they had to take their discoveries to a higher authority to ensure proper protection and oversight. They decided to present their findings to the Royal Society of Engineers, an esteemed body known for its commitment to innovation and ethical standards.

The presentation was a momentous occasion. Danny, Eleanor, Victor, and Hawthorne stood before the Society's distinguished members, sharing their journey, discoveries, and the challenges they had faced. They demonstrated the engine's capabilities, the key's control mechanisms, and the potential of the rare mineral.

The members of the Society were awed and deeply impressed. After a thorough review, they agreed to support Danny and his team, providing resources and protection to further their research and ensure the technology was used responsibly.

As the meeting concluded, Danny felt a sense of relief and accomplishment. They had not only protected the ancient steam engine but had also laid the groundwork for a future where its power could be harnessed for the greater good.

Returning to their workshop, they found a new sense of purpose and camaraderie. The challenges ahead were still daunting, but they faced them with confidence and a united front.

One evening, as they gathered around the workshop table, Danny looked at his friends and allies, gratitude and determination shining in his eyes. "We've come a long way, and there's still much to do. But I believe we're on the right path. Together, we can ensure that this technology brings light and progress to our world."

Eleanor, Victor, and Hawthorne nodded in agreement, their faces reflecting the same resolve. They raised their glasses in a toast, the clinking sound echoing through the workshop.

"To the future," Danny said, his voice filled with hope. "And to the legacy we'll leave behind."

As the night deepened and the stars shone brightly above, the team continued their work, driven by the knowledge that they were part of something much larger than themselves. The ancient steam engine was more than just a marvel of engineering—it was a beacon of possibility, a testament to human ingenuity and the relentless pursuit of progress.

Chapter Six: Second Incident

The sense of accomplishment that had settled over Danny and his team was soon disrupted by yet another strange occurrence. It started one evening, as they were preparing to retire for the night. A loud clanging noise echoed through the workshop, followed by the sound of machinery grinding to a halt.

Danny and Eleanor exchanged worried glances. "What now?" Danny muttered, heading towards the source of the commotion.

In the corner of the workshop, an automaton—one of Danny's earlier creations—had come to life on its own. Its eyes glowed with an unnatural light, and its movements were jerky and erratic. Sparks flew from its joints, and it emitted a series of high-pitched whistles and clicks.

Danny approached cautiously, his mind racing. "This automaton has been decommissioned for months. How is it moving?"

Eleanor, her curiosity piqued, began to examine the automaton's internal mechanisms. "It's as if it's been reactivated by an external power source," she said, her brow furrowing in concentration. "But I can't figure out how."

Victor joined them, his face grim. "Could this be related to the steam engine? If the engine's power can affect the village's power grid, it might also be influencing other machinery."

Danny nodded. "It's possible. We need to shut it down before it causes any more damage."

With precise movements, Danny disabled the automaton, carefully removing its power core and disconnecting its circuits. The machine fell silent, its eyes dimming to darkness. He placed the components on the workbench, deep in thought.

"We need to investigate further," Danny said, turning to his team. "If the steam engine's power is influencing other devices, we could be dealing with a much larger problem."

Eleanor suggested they check the workshop's power systems and the surrounding area for any unusual activity. Using the steam analyzer, they detected faint traces of the same energy signature they had observed in the ancient steam engine. The readings led them to a small, hidden compartment in the workshop's foundation, where they discovered a series of old wires and circuits connected to a mysterious device.

"This must have been part of my great-grandfather's original setup," Danny said, examining the device. "It looks like it was designed to harness the engine's power and distribute it throughout the workshop."

Hawthorne, who had been studying the journal, joined them. "William Martin's notes mentioned a network of devices meant to channel the engine's energy. This could be one of those devices, reactivated by the recent events."

As they worked to disable the device, a sudden realization struck Danny. "If there are more of these devices scattered throughout the village, they could be causing all sorts of malfunctions."

Victor nodded. "We need to find and neutralize them before they cause any more disruptions."

Over the next few days, the team scoured the village, using the steam analyzer to detect any anomalies. They found several more hidden devices, each one intricately connected to the village's power grid and machinery. It became clear that William Martin had created a sophisticated network to experiment with the steam engine's energy.

During their search, they encountered another malfunctioning automaton, this one more aggressive and dangerous. It had been part of a local factory's assembly line, and its erratic behavior had caused significant damage to the production process. The factory workers were terrified, unsure of how to handle the rogue machine.

Danny, Eleanor, and Victor arrived at the factory to assess the situation. The automaton was thrashing wildly, its movements unpredictable and violent. Danny approached cautiously, his tools at the ready.

"We need to shut it down before it hurts someone," he said, signaling to Eleanor and Victor to flank the automaton.

As they moved into position, the automaton suddenly turned its glowing eyes towards Danny and lunged. Danny narrowly avoided its grasp, using his agility and quick reflexes to stay out of reach. Eleanor managed to get behind the automaton and began to disable its power core, while Victor used a steam-powered net launcher to entangle its limbs.

With coordinated effort, they managed to subdue the automaton and shut it down. The factory workers cheered, grateful for their intervention.

Back at the workshop, they analyzed the automaton's components and found the same energy signature as the previous one. "This confirms it," Danny said. "The steam engine's power is somehow affecting these machines. We need to find a way to contain it."

Eleanor suggested they create a series of dampening fields around the affected areas, using modified versions of the key's control mechanisms. "If we can isolate the energy and prevent it from spreading, we can reduce the risk of further malfunctions."

Victor agreed. "We should also enhance the security around the steam engine itself. If someone is trying to harness its power, we need to make sure they can't access it."

Working together, they designed and built the dampening fields, strategically placing them around the village and in key locations within the workshop. The fields successfully reduced the instances of erratic behavior in the machinery, providing a temporary solution to the problem.

However, Danny knew that they needed a more permanent fix. He delved deeper into his great-grandfather's journal, searching for any additional clues. One entry caught his eye:

"March 5, 1882: The key must be used in conjunction with a stabilizing device, one that can regulate the flow of energy and prevent disruptions. I have hidden the blueprints for this device in a secure location, known only to my descendants."

Danny's heart raced as he read the entry. "We need to find these blueprints. They could hold the key to permanently stabilizing the steam engine's power."

Eleanor and Victor looked at him with renewed determination. "Where do we start?" Eleanor asked.

Danny thought for a moment, then recalled a conversation he had once had with his father about a hidden study in their old family estate. "There's a study in my family's estate, passed down through generations. My father mentioned it was a place where our ancestors kept their most valuable secrets. That's where we'll find the blueprints."

They set off for the Martin family estate, a grand old mansion on the outskirts of the city. The estate had been abandoned for years, its halls filled with dust and echoes of the past. Danny led them through the creaking corridors to a hidden door concealed behind a bookshelf in the library.

With a sense of anticipation, he pushed the door open, revealing a small, dimly lit study. The room was filled with old books, maps, and artifacts. In the center of the room was a large oak desk, and on it, a sealed envelope bearing the Martin family crest.

Danny carefully opened the envelope and pulled out a set of blueprints. His great-grandfather's precise handwriting covered the pages, detailing the design of the stabilizing device. "This is it," Danny said, his voice filled with awe. "These blueprints will help us control the engine's power once and for all."

As they pored over the blueprints, Eleanor's eyes lit up with excitement. "This device is ingenious. It uses a series of harmonic resonators to regulate the flow of energy, ensuring stability and preventing surges."

Victor examined the design closely. "We'll need to gather the necessary materials and start building immediately. The sooner we have this device in place, the better."

Back at the workshop, they worked tirelessly, assembling the components and fine-tuning the design. The process was complex and challenging, but their combined expertise and determination saw them through.

Finally, after days of relentless effort, the stabilizing device was complete. They transported it to the underground chamber and carefully integrated it with the ancient steam engine. As they activated the device, a soft hum filled the air, and the engine's erratic pulses smoothed into a steady, controlled rhythm.

Eleanor monitored the energy readings, her face breaking into a smile. "It's working. The energy is stable, and the dampening fields are no longer necessary."

Danny felt a wave of relief wash over him. "We've done it. The engine is under control."

Victor placed a hand on Danny's shoulder. "This is a significant achievement, Danny. Your great-grandfather would be proud."

Hawthorne, who had been observing their progress, nodded in agreement. "You've not only secured the engine's power but also ensured it can be used for the betterment of society. This is a legacy worth preserving."

As they stood together, the weight of their accomplishment sinking in, Danny felt a renewed sense of purpose.

Chapter Seven: Meeting Allies

In the days following their successful stabilization of the steam engine, Danny and his team knew their work was far from over. The ancient engine, while now under control, held many secrets yet to be uncovered. To further their research, Danny decided to bring in additional expertise. He reached out to Professor Thaddeus Harkness, a renowned historian with a deep knowledge of ancient technologies, and Evelyn Gearspring, a skilled mechanic known for her innovative approaches to mechanical engineering.

Professor Harkness arrived first, a distinguished figure with sharp eyes that seemed to miss nothing. His presence brought an air of scholarly gravitas to the workshop. He meticulously examined the blueprints, journals, and the engine itself, drawing on his extensive knowledge to provide valuable insights.

"This engine," Harkness mused, adjusting his spectacles, "is not just a piece of advanced technology. It is a culmination of centuries of knowledge, possibly even drawing from lost civilizations. Your great-grandfather was on the brink of uncovering something truly monumental."

Evelyn Gearspring soon followed, her arrival marked by the clatter of tools and a confident stride. Her practical expertise complemented Harkness's theoretical insights perfectly. She dove into the technical aspects of the engine, her hands deftly adjusting and improving its components.

"I can see why this engine caused so much trouble," Evelyn said, her voice filled with excitement. "It's designed to channel immense power, but it needs fine-tuning to handle the energy safely. With some adjustments, we can optimize its efficiency and stability."

The expanded team quickly found a rhythm, each member contributing their unique skills and perspectives. Danny, Eleanor, Victor, Harkness, and Evelyn formed a formidable group, united by their common goal.

One evening, as they gathered around the workshop table, Professor Harkness presented his latest findings. "I've been analyzing the journal and cross-referencing it with historical texts. It seems your great-grandfather discovered references to an ancient society known as the Ordo Mechanica, which possessed advanced knowledge of steam power and mechanical engineering."

Danny leaned in, intrigued. "The Ordo Mechanica? I've never heard of them."

Harkness nodded. "They were a secretive order, believed to have been wiped out centuries ago. However, their knowledge survived in fragments, passed down through generations of inventors and scholars. William Martin may have tapped into this legacy, and his work on the engine is a continuation of their discoveries."

Evelyn, her hands busy with a small mechanical device, looked up. "So, we're dealing with knowledge that spans centuries, possibly even millennia. No wonder this engine is so advanced. If we can fully understand it, we might unlock a new era of technological progress."

Their excitement was palpable as they delved deeper into the mysteries of the Ordo Mechanica. Harkness's research led them to an old manuscript hidden in the library of a nearby university. The manuscript, written in a mix of Latin and obscure symbols, contained detailed descriptions of the order's inventions and philosophies.

Translating the manuscript was a painstaking process, but Harkness's expertise and Eleanor's linguistic skills made steady progress. The manuscript revealed plans for several advanced machines, including a prototype for a perpetual motion device and an automated city powered entirely by steam.

Meanwhile, Evelyn focused on improving the engine's design. She incorporated modern materials and techniques, enhancing its performance and safety. Her modifications made the engine more efficient, reducing the risk of future malfunctions.

One night, as they worked late into the evening, a sense of unease settled over the workshop. Danny couldn't shake the feeling that they were being watched. He mentioned his concerns to Victor, who immediately took steps to increase security around the workshop.

Victor's precautions proved timely. The following night, a group of intruders attempted to break into the workshop, seeking to steal the engine and the knowledge they had uncovered. Thanks to Victor's foresight, they were able to fend off the attack and secure their work.

The incident reinforced their resolve to protect their discoveries. They redoubled their efforts, determined to uncover the full potential of the ancient steam engine while ensuring it remained out of the wrong hands.

As days turned into weeks, their progress was remarkable. The manuscript revealed a hidden location where the Ordo Mechanica had stored their most prized inventions. It was a remote, mountainous region, accessible only by a treacherous path.

Danny and his team prepared for the journey, gathering supplies and reinforcing their defenses. They knew the risks were great, but the potential rewards were too significant to ignore.

The journey to the hidden location was arduous. They traveled by steam-powered carriage, navigating narrow, winding roads and steep cliffs. Along the way, they encountered various challenges, from mechanical failures to treacherous weather.

Despite these obstacles, their determination never wavered. They finally reached a secluded valley, where they discovered an ancient, overgrown entrance carved into the mountainside. The entrance bore the symbol of the Ordo Mechanica, confirming they had found the right place.

Inside, they discovered a vast underground complex filled with ancient machinery and intricate carvings. The air was thick with the scent of oil and metal, and the faint hum of long-dormant machines echoed through the halls.

Professor Harkness led the way, his eyes wide with wonder. "This is incredible. It's like stepping into a forgotten world. The Ordo Mechanica's knowledge has been preserved here for centuries."

Evelyn, her eyes scanning the machinery, was equally impressed. "These machines are like nothing I've ever seen. If we can understand and replicate them, it could revolutionize our technology."

They carefully explored the complex, documenting their findings and collecting samples of the ancient materials. The more they uncovered, the clearer it became that the Ordo Mechanica had been far ahead of their time.

Danny, meanwhile, focused on the central chamber, where they discovered a massive, ornate machine that seemed to be the heart of the complex. Its design was similar to the ancient steam engine, but on a grander scale.

"This must be the source of the Ordo Mechanica's power," Danny said, his voice filled with awe. "If we can activate it, we might unlock even greater potential."

With Harkness's guidance and Evelyn's mechanical expertise, they began to decipher the machine's workings. It was a complex process, requiring a delicate balance of skill and intuition.

As they worked, they uncovered more about the Ordo Mechanica's philosophy. The order had believed in the harmonious integration of man and machine, seeking to use their knowledge for the betterment of society.

Their efforts paid off when they finally succeeded in activating the machine. It sprang to life with a deep, resonant hum, filling the chamber with a warm, golden light. The power it generated was immense, yet controlled and stable.

Eleanor monitored the energy readings, her face lighting up with excitement. "This is it. We've unlocked the true potential of the Ordo Mechanica's knowledge."

Danny felt a surge of pride and hope. They had come so far and uncovered so much, but he knew their journey was just beginning. With the ancient knowledge of the Ordo Mechanica and the advancements they had made, they were on the brink of a new era of technological progress.

Chapter Eight: Uncovering Secrets

With the central machine of the Ordo Mechanica complex activated, the team felt an exhilarating rush of possibility. Yet, their exploration was far from over. Their attention turned to a series of ornate doors at the far end of the chamber. These doors, engraved with intricate patterns and symbols, seemed to beckon them forward.

As they approached, Professor Harkness carefully examined the inscriptions. "These symbols tell a story," he murmured, tracing his fingers over the carvings. "It seems to depict the history of the Ordo Mechanica and their journey to mastering steam technology."

Evelyn, ever curious, pushed one of the doors open. The group stepped inside, their lanterns casting long shadows on the stone walls. They found themselves in a hidden laboratory, preserved in time. Ancient relics and documents lay scattered across workbenches, and the air was thick with the scent of aged parchment and metal.

"This is incredible," Danny said, his voice filled with wonder. "It's like stepping into the past."

Harkness approached a large, dust-covered table in the center of the room. He carefully cleared away the debris, revealing a collection of detailed schematics and journals. "These documents could hold the key to understanding the true origins of steam technology."

Eleanor picked up a fragile manuscript, its pages yellowed with age. As she carefully turned the pages, she gasped. "These writings predate even the Ordo Mechanica. They mention an even older civilization that first harnessed the power of steam."

The manuscript described a society known as the Pneumarians, who lived thousands of years ago. The Pneumarians were said to have discovered a rare mineral deep within the earth, which they used to generate steam power. Their technology was advanced, allowing them to build magnificent cities and machines.

Danny's eyes widened as he read over Eleanor's shoulder. "This mineral—it's the same one we found in the engine. The Pneumarians must have been the true originators of steam technology."

Evelyn, examining a set of blueprints, found references to ancient steam engines far more sophisticated than anything they had seen before. "These designs are incredible. If we can understand and replicate them, it could revolutionize everything we know about steam power."

As they delved deeper into the laboratory, they uncovered more relics and documents that painted a vivid picture of the Pneumarians' achievements. They found intricate models of steam-powered machines, maps of ancient cities, and even a set of crystals that seemed to resonate with a strange energy.

Professor Harkness studied the crystals intently. "These must be the source of the Pneumarians' power. If we can learn how to harness their energy, it could open up new possibilities for our technology."

Their excitement was tempered by the realization that the Pneumarians had ultimately disappeared, leaving only their relics behind. The documents hinted at a great catastrophe, possibly linked to their overreliance on steam power.

"We need to be careful," Danny said, his tone serious. "The Pneumarians' technology is powerful, but it also comes with great risks. We must learn from their mistakes."

Eleanor nodded in agreement. "We should focus on understanding the limits of this technology and finding ways to use it responsibly."

As they continued to explore the laboratory, they discovered a hidden chamber containing a large, ornate box. Inside, they found a pristine steam engine, unlike anything they had seen before. It was smaller and more refined, with a design that suggested incredible efficiency and power.

"This must be a prototype," Evelyn said, her eyes shining with excitement. "If we can figure out how it works, it could be the key to unlocking the full potential of steam technology."

They carefully transported the prototype back to their workshop, eager to begin their analysis. Back at the workshop, they laid out all the documents, relics, and the prototype engine. The team split up, each focusing on different aspects of their findings.

Professor Harkness continued translating the ancient manuscripts, uncovering more about the Pneumarians' society and their technological advancements. He found references to a vast network of steam-powered cities, connected by underground tunnels and transport systems.

Evelyn dissected the prototype engine, marveling at its intricate design. "This is a masterpiece of engineering," she said, her voice filled with admiration. "The components are perfectly balanced, and the efficiency is unmatched. If we can replicate this on a larger scale, it could change everything."

Danny, meanwhile, focused on integrating the new knowledge with their existing work on the ancient steam engine. He discovered that many of the Pneumarians' principles could be applied to improve the engine's performance and safety.

One evening, as they worked late into the night, a sudden realization struck Danny. "The crystals," he said, his eyes lighting up. "They're the key to everything. If we can understand how to harness their energy, we can unlock the true potential of steam power."

Harkness nodded. "The Pneumarians used these crystals as a sustainable energy source. They must have developed methods to control and utilize their power safely."

Eleanor suggested they set up a series of experiments to study the crystals and their properties. "We need to understand how they interact with the steam engines and how we can replicate the Pneumarians' techniques."

The team set to work, designing and conducting experiments with the crystals. They discovered that the crystals emitted a unique form of energy that could be harnessed to generate steam more efficiently than traditional methods. By carefully calibrating the energy output, they could create a stable and powerful steam source.

As their understanding grew, they began to incorporate the crystals into their designs. The prototype engine, once modified with the crystal energy source, performed beyond their wildest expectations. It ran smoothly and efficiently, with no signs of the instability that had plagued their earlier efforts.

Evelyn couldn't contain her excitement. "This is it! We've found the key to a new era of steam technology. With these crystals, we can create machines that are more powerful and efficient than ever before."

Their breakthrough attracted the attention of the Royal Society of Engineers once again. The Society recognized the potential of their discovery and offered to provide additional resources and support to further their research.

With the backing of the Royal Society, Danny and his team expanded their efforts. They began to design larger, more ambitious projects, incorporating the crystal-powered engines into everything from transportation systems to industrial machinery.

As they worked, they remained mindful of the lessons they had learned from the Pneumarians. They implemented strict safety protocols and conducted thorough testing to ensure their technology was used responsibly.

Despite their progress, they faced new challenges and mysteries. The ancient manuscripts hinted at even greater secrets, hidden in lost cities and forgotten archives.

Chapter Nine: Breakthrough

The workshop was bathed in the golden glow of gas lamps as Danny, Eleanor, Victor, Professor Harkness, and Evelyn Gearspring pored over the ancient manuscripts and blueprints scattered across the large oak table. The air hummed with the excitement of recent discoveries, but a new enigma had captured their attention: a coded message inscribed on the back of one of the Pneumarian blueprints.

Danny held the blueprint up to the light, his eyes narrowing as he studied the intricate symbols and patterns. "This message is different from anything we've seen before. It's almost like a puzzle, meant to be deciphered."

Eleanor leaned in, her curiosity piqued. "What does it say, Danny?"

"It's hard to tell," Danny replied, running a hand through his hair. "But it seems to be pointing to a specific location. If we can decode it, we might find the source of the ancient steam engine's immense power."

Professor Harkness adjusted his spectacles, scrutinizing the symbols. "These symbols are a combination of ancient languages and ciphers. It will take time to decode, but I believe we can do it."

Evelyn, ever the problem solver, offered, "Let's break it down systematically. We can cross-reference the symbols with what we've already translated from the manuscripts."

The team worked late into the night, their minds focused on the task at hand. Danny felt a surge of determination. They were on the verge of uncovering something monumental, and he could almost feel the answers slipping into place.

Hours later, as the first light of dawn began to creep through the workshop windows, Danny exclaimed, "I've got it!" The others gathered around, their eyes wide with anticipation.

"The message is a set of coordinates," Danny explained, pointing to a series of numbers and letters on the blueprint. "It leads to a remote location in the mountains, a place called the Valley of Echoes. According to this, that's where we'll find the source of the steam engine's power."

Victor raised an eyebrow. "The Valley of Echoes? I've heard legends about that place. It's said to be filled with strange phenomena and ancient ruins."

Professor Harkness nodded. "The Valley of Echoes has always been shrouded in mystery. If the Pneumarians chose it as the location for their most powerful engine, it makes sense."

Evelyn's eyes sparkled with excitement. "Then what are we waiting for? Let's prepare for the journey."

The team wasted no time gathering their supplies and readying their steam-powered carriage for the trip. They knew the journey would be challenging, but the promise of discovering the true source of the steam engine's power drove them forward.

The journey to the Valley of Echoes was arduous. The narrow, winding roads were treacherous, and the steep cliffs offered breathtaking views that were both beautiful and intimidating. The steam-powered carriage chugged along, its engine humming steadily as it climbed higher into the mountains.

As they neared their destination, the landscape grew more rugged, and the air was filled with an eerie stillness. The valley itself was nestled between towering peaks, its entrance marked by a series of ancient stone pillars covered in strange symbols.

"This must be the place," Danny said, his voice hushed with awe. "The Valley of Echoes."

They disembarked from the carriage and made their way into the valley, their footsteps echoing eerily off the stone walls. The air was thick with the scent of damp earth and moss, and the only sound was the distant rumble of a waterfall.

Eleanor examined the stone pillars, tracing the symbols with her fingers. "These markings are similar to the ones we found on the blueprint. We're definitely in the right place."

As they ventured deeper into the valley, they came across a series of ancient ruins, partially hidden by overgrown vegetation. The ruins were a testament to the Pneumarians' architectural prowess, with towering stone structures and intricate carvings that seemed to tell a story of a long-lost civilization.

Professor Harkness, his eyes wide with wonder, remarked, "This is extraordinary. These ruins are in remarkably good condition for their age. It's as if the valley has protected them from the ravages of time."

Evelyn, her mechanical expertise never far from her thoughts, inspected a series of old, rusted gears embedded in one of the stone structures. "These mechanisms are ancient, but they look like they were part of a larger machine. I wonder if they were connected to the steam engine."

Danny's attention was drawn to a large, ornate door at the center of the ruins. The door was made of a strange, dark metal, and it was covered in the same symbols they had seen on the blueprint. He approached it cautiously, feeling a mixture of excitement and trepidation.

"This door looks like it leads to something important," Danny said, examining the symbols. "It might be the entrance to the chamber where the steam engine is housed."

Victor stepped forward, his hand resting on the hilt of his steam-powered weapon. "Let's open it and find out."

With a collective effort, they pushed the heavy door open, revealing a dark passageway that led deep into the heart of the mountain. The passage was lined with glowing crystals that emitted a soft, eerie light, casting long shadows on the stone walls.

The team proceeded cautiously, their lanterns casting flickering beams of light ahead of them. As they ventured deeper into the passage, the air grew warmer, and the hum of machinery became more pronounced.

Finally, they emerged into a vast underground chamber, and what they saw took their breath away. In the center of the chamber stood the ancient steam engine, an awe-inspiring construct of brass, steel, and glowing crystals. It was larger and more intricate than anything they had ever seen, its components humming with untapped power.

Eleanor's eyes widened in amazement. "This engine is incredible. It's unlike anything we've ever encountered."

Professor Harkness approached the engine with reverence. "This is the culmination of the Pneumarians' knowledge and ingenuity. It's the true source of their power."

Evelyn began to examine the engine's components, her hands moving deftly over the intricate machinery. "The design is ingenious. The crystals are integrated into the engine in a way that maximizes their energy output. It's no wonder this engine is so powerful."

Danny, feeling a sense of destiny, approached a large control panel at the base of the engine. The panel was covered in symbols and dials, each one meticulously designed to control the flow of energy.

"We need to figure out how to activate the engine and harness its power," Danny said, his voice filled with determination.

Victor, ever the protector, kept a watchful eye on their surroundings. "We should be cautious. We don't know what might happen when we activate it."

As they worked together to decipher the control panel, they felt the weight of history on their shoulders. The Pneumarians had entrusted their greatest creation to the Valley of Echoes, and now it was up to Danny and his team to unlock its potential.

Hours passed as they carefully adjusted the dials and inputted the symbols they had deciphered from the manuscripts. Finally, with a deep, resonant hum, the engine sprang to life. The chamber was filled with a warm, golden light, and the air vibrated with energy.

Eleanor monitored the energy readings, her face lighting up with excitement. "The energy output is stable and controlled. We've done it!"

Evelyn couldn't contain her joy. "This is a game-changer. With this engine, we can revolutionize steam technology."

Professor Harkness, his eyes shining with pride, added, "We've uncovered the true legacy of the Pneumarians. This engine is a testament to their brilliance and vision."

Danny, feeling a profound sense of accomplishment, looked at his team. "We've come so far, and there's still so much to learn. This is just the beginning."

As they stood together, bathed in the golden light of the ancient steam engine, they knew that their journey was far from over. The mysteries of the Valley of Echoes and the Pneumarians' technology awaited them, and with each step forward, they moved closer to unlocking the full potential of the steam engine and its immense, untapped power.

Chapter Ten: Confrontation with Blackwell

The workshop was bathed in the golden glow of gas lamps as Danny, Eleanor, Victor, Professor Harkness, and Evelyn Gearspring pored over the ancient manuscripts and blueprints scattered across the large oak table. The air hummed with the excitement of recent discoveries, but a new enigma had captured their attention: a coded message inscribed on the back of one of the Pneumarian blueprints.

Danny held the blueprint up to the light, his eyes narrowing as he studied the intricate symbols and patterns. "This message is different from anything we've seen before. It's almost like a puzzle, meant to be deciphered."

Eleanor leaned in, her curiosity piqued. "What does it say, Danny?"

"It's hard to tell," Danny replied, running a hand through his hair. "But it seems to be pointing to a specific location. If we can decode it, we might find the source of the ancient steam engine's immense power."

Professor Harkness adjusted his spectacles, scrutinizing the symbols. "These symbols are a combination of ancient languages and ciphers. It will take time to decode, but I believe we can do it."

Evelyn, ever the problem solver, offered, "Let's break it down systematically. We can cross-reference the symbols with what we've already translated from the manuscripts."

The team worked late into the night, their minds focused on the task at hand. Danny felt a surge of determination. They were on the verge of uncovering something monumental, and he could almost feel the answers slipping into place.

Hours later, as the first light of dawn began to creep through the workshop windows, Danny exclaimed, "I've got it!" The others gathered around, their eyes wide with anticipation.

"The message is a set of coordinates," Danny explained, pointing to a series of numbers and letters on the blueprint. "It leads to a remote location in the mountains, a place called the Valley of Echoes. According to this, that's where we'll find the source of the steam engine's power."

Victor raised an eyebrow. "The Valley of Echoes? I've heard legends about that place. It's said to be filled with strange phenomena and ancient ruins."

Professor Harkness nodded. "The Valley of Echoes has always been shrouded in mystery. If the Pneumarians chose it as the location for their most powerful engine, it makes sense."

Evelyn's eyes sparkled with excitement. "Then what are we waiting for? Let's prepare for the journey."

The team wasted no time gathering their supplies and readying their steam-powered carriage for the trip. They knew the journey would be challenging, but the promise of discovering the true source of the steam engine's power drove them forward.

The journey to the Valley of Echoes was arduous. The narrow, winding roads were treacherous, and the steep cliffs offered breathtaking views that were both beautiful and intimidating. The steam-powered carriage chugged along, its engine humming steadily as it climbed higher into the mountains.

As they neared their destination, the landscape grew more rugged, and the air was filled with an eerie stillness. The valley itself was nestled between towering peaks, its entrance marked by a series of ancient stone pillars covered in strange symbols.

"This must be the place," Danny said, his voice hushed with awe. "The Valley of Echoes."

They disembarked from the carriage and made their way into the valley, their footsteps echoing eerily off the stone walls. The air was thick with the scent of damp earth and moss, and the only sound was the distant rumble of a waterfall.

Eleanor examined the stone pillars, tracing the symbols with her fingers. "These markings are similar to the ones we found on the blueprint. We're definitely in the right place."

As they ventured deeper into the valley, they came across a series of ancient ruins, partially hidden by overgrown vegetation. The ruins were a testament to the Pneumarians' architectural prowess, with towering stone structures and intricate carvings that seemed to tell a story of a long-lost civilization.

Professor Harkness, his eyes wide with wonder, remarked, "This is extraordinary. These ruins are in remarkably good condition for their age. It's as if the valley has protected them from the ravages of time."

Evelyn, her mechanical expertise never far from her thoughts, inspected a series of old, rusted gears embedded in one of the stone structures. "These mechanisms are ancient, but they look like they were part of a larger machine. I wonder if they were connected to the steam engine."

Danny's attention was drawn to a large, ornate door at the center of the ruins. The door was made of a strange, dark metal, and it was covered in the same symbols they had seen on the blueprint. He approached it cautiously, feeling a mixture of excitement and trepidation.

"This door looks like it leads to something important," Danny said, examining the symbols. "It might be the entrance to the chamber where the steam engine is housed."

Victor stepped forward, his hand resting on the hilt of his steam-powered weapon. "Let's open it and find out."

With a collective effort, they pushed the heavy door open, revealing a dark passageway that led deep into the heart of the mountain. The passage was lined with glowing crystals that emitted a soft, eerie light, casting long shadows on the stone walls.

The team proceeded cautiously, their lanterns casting flickering beams of light ahead of them. As they ventured deeper into the passage, the air grew warmer, and the hum of machinery became more pronounced.

Finally, they emerged into a vast underground chamber, and what they saw took their breath away. In the center of the chamber stood the ancient steam engine, an awe-inspiring construct of brass, steel, and glowing crystals. It was larger and more intricate than anything they had ever seen, its components humming with untapped power.

Eleanor's eyes widened in amazement. "This engine is incredible. It's unlike anything we've ever encountered."

Professor Harkness approached the engine with reverence. "This is the culmination of the Pneumarians' knowledge and ingenuity. It's the true source of their power."

Evelyn began to examine the engine's components, her hands moving deftly over the intricate machinery. "The design is ingenious. The crystals are integrated into the engine in a way that maximizes their energy output. It's no wonder this engine is so powerful."

Danny, feeling a sense of destiny, approached a large control panel at the base of the engine. The panel was covered in symbols and dials, each one meticulously designed to control the flow of energy.

"We need to figure out how to activate the engine and harness its power," Danny said, his voice filled with determination.

Victor, ever the protector, kept a watchful eye on their surroundings. "We should be cautious. We don't know what might happen when we activate it."

As they worked together to decipher the control panel, they felt the weight of history on their shoulders. The Pneumarians had entrusted their greatest creation to the Valley of Echoes, and now it was up to Danny and his team to unlock its potential.

Hours passed as they carefully adjusted the dials and inputted the symbols they had deciphered from the manuscripts. Finally, with a deep, resonant hum, the engine sprang to life. The chamber was filled with a warm, golden light, and the air vibrated with energy.

Eleanor monitored the energy readings, her face lighting up with excitement. "The energy output is stable and controlled. We've done it!"

Evelyn couldn't contain her joy. "This is a game-changer. With this engine, we can revolutionize steam technology."

Professor Harkness, his eyes shining with pride, added, "We've uncovered the true legacy of the Pneumarians. This engine is a testament to their brilliance and vision."

Danny, feeling a profound sense of accomplishment, looked at his team. "We've come so far, and there's still so much to learn. This is just the beginning."

As they stood together, bathed in the golden light of the ancient steam engine, they knew that their journey was far from over. The mysteries of the Valley of Echoes and the Pneumarians' technology awaited them, and with each step forward, they moved closer to unlocking the full potential of the steam engine and its immense, untapped power.

The euphoria of their discovery in the Valley of Echoes was abruptly shattered when Danny's communication device buzzed urgently. He quickly answered, and a frantic voice on the other end filled the chamber.

"Danny! It's Steven from the workshop. You need to get back immediately. It's Lord Blackwell—he's found out about the engine, and he's mobilizing his forces. He plans to seize it for himself!"

Danny's heart sank. Lord Blackwell was a notorious industrialist, known for his ruthless tactics and insatiable hunger for power. If he managed to harness the steam engine's immense energy, the consequences could be catastrophic.

"We need to get back to the workshop," Danny said, his voice steady despite the urgency. "We can't let Blackwell take the engine."

The team quickly gathered their equipment and made their way back to the entrance of the Valley of Echoes. The journey back to the workshop was tense, each mile filled with a growing sense of urgency. The steam-powered carriage pushed its limits, racing against time and the threat looming over their discovery.

As they neared the workshop, they saw smoke rising in the distance and heard the clanging of metal and shouts of confrontation. Blackwell's men were already there, attempting to breach the reinforced doors of the workshop.

Danny, Victor, and Evelyn disembarked first, with Professor Harkness and Eleanor close behind. They approached cautiously, assessing the situation.

Victor tightened his grip on his steam-powered weapon. "We need to find a way to stop them before they break through."

Evelyn nodded, already formulating a plan. "I can create a diversion with some of the equipment in the carriage. It should buy us some time to get inside and secure the engine."

Danny agreed. "Do it. We'll use the distraction to slip past them and fortify the workshop from the inside."

Evelyn set to work, rigging a series of small, steam-powered devices that would create loud noises and flashes of light. When she was ready, she activated the devices, and the area erupted in chaos. Blackwell's men, caught off guard, scrambled to understand what was happening.

Using the distraction to their advantage, Danny and the others slipped past the confused guards and into the workshop. Once inside, they quickly bolted the doors and reinforced them with whatever they could find.

Steven, the workshop assistant, was there, his face pale with worry. "Danny, they're after the engine. They know how powerful it is."

"We know, Steven," Danny said, gripping his shoulder. "We need to protect it at all costs. Help us fortify the entrances and secure the engine."

As they worked, the clamor outside intensified. Blackwell's men were regrouping, and it was only a matter of time before they would attempt another assault. The workshop, usually a place of creation and innovation, had become a battleground.

Danny turned to his team, his face set with determination. "We need a plan to confront Blackwell directly. If we can't stop him here, he'll keep coming back."

Victor, ever the strategist, suggested, "We could use the engine's power to create a defensive perimeter. It's risky, but it might be our best shot."

Eleanor and Professor Harkness agreed. "If we can harness the engine's energy, we can create a barrier that will keep Blackwell's men at bay," Harkness explained. "But it will require precise control."

Evelyn nodded. "I can modify the engine's output to generate a protective field. But we'll need to act quickly."

As Evelyn and Harkness worked on the engine, Danny and Victor prepared for the confrontation. They knew that the barrier would only buy them time; ultimately, they would need to face Blackwell himself.

Minutes later, the workshop shook as Blackwell's men launched another assault. The reinforced doors creaked and groaned under the pressure. Evelyn activated the modified steam engine, and a shimmering energy field enveloped the workshop, repelling the attackers and buying them crucial time.

Outside, Lord Blackwell himself stepped forward, his imposing figure flanked by heavily armed guards. His eyes were cold and calculating as he surveyed the scene. "Danny Martin!" he called out, his voice booming. "You cannot hide forever. Surrender the engine to me, and I might spare your lives."

Danny stepped out of the workshop, his heart pounding but his resolve unshaken. "Blackwell, this engine isn't yours to take. It's too powerful to be in the hands of someone like you."

Blackwell sneered, his lips curling into a cruel smile. "You're a fool, Danny. This engine is the key to unimaginable power. With it, I can reshape the world as I see fit. Stand aside, or face the consequences."

Victor and Evelyn joined Danny, their expressions defiant. "We won't let you take it," Victor said firmly. "We'll fight to protect it."

Blackwell's eyes narrowed. "So be it. Men, prepare to breach the barrier!"

As Blackwell's forces moved to attack, Danny and his allies braced themselves. The energy field flickered and pulsed, holding strong against the initial onslaught. But Danny knew it wouldn't last forever.

Inside the workshop, Eleanor and Professor Harkness continued to monitor the engine. "The field is holding, but it's under immense strain," Eleanor reported. "We need to find a way to strengthen it."

Harkness nodded, deep in thought. "Perhaps if we can amplify the crystal's output..."

Suddenly, the barrier shuddered, and a loud explosion rocked the workshop. Blackwell's men had breached the perimeter, and the energy field was failing. Danny, Victor, and Evelyn prepared to make their stand.

Blackwell advanced, his guards flanking him, weapons at the ready. "This is your last chance, Danny," he warned. "Surrender the engine, or face annihilation."

Danny stood his ground, his eyes blazing with determination. "We'll never surrender. This engine is meant to benefit humanity, not serve your twisted ambitions."

With a roar, Blackwell's men surged forward, and the battle began in earnest. The workshop became a flurry of movement and sound, with steam-powered weapons clashing and the hum of machinery filling the air.

Victor fought valiantly, his steam-powered gauntlets delivering powerful blows to any attacker who came too close. Evelyn used her mechanical expertise to create improvised traps and defenses, slowing down Blackwell's advance.

Danny, fueled by a fierce determination to protect their discovery, faced off against Blackwell himself. The two clashed, their battle a contest of wills as much as strength. Blackwell's greed and ambition against Danny's resolve and sense of justice.

"You're out of your depth, Martin," Blackwell sneered as they fought. "You think you can stop me? I've crushed greater men than you."

Danny parried a blow and countered with one of his own, his eyes never leaving Blackwell's. "This isn't about me. It's about doing what's right. And I won't let you corrupt this power."

The battle raged on, each side giving their all. Inside the workshop, Eleanor and Harkness worked frantically to stabilize the engine and find a way to reinforce the failing barrier. The air was thick with tension and the acrid smell of steam and metal.

As the fight reached its climax, Blackwell landed a heavy blow on Danny, knocking him to the ground. He stood over Danny, his eyes gleaming with triumph. "It's over, Martin. You've lost."

But just as Blackwell raised his weapon for the final strike, a sudden surge of energy erupted from the engine. The barrier flared brightly, and a shockwave rippled through the workshop, knocking everyone off their feet.

Danny, seizing the moment, scrambled to his feet and tackled Blackwell, disarming him with a swift, decisive move. The two men grappled, the outcome hanging in the balance.

Inside, Eleanor and Harkness managed to stabilize the engine, channeling its energy into a focused beam that repelled Blackwell's men and reinforced the barrier. The tide of the battle was turning.

Victor and Evelyn joined Danny, helping to subdue Blackwell and secure the workshop. With their leader captured and the barrier restored, Blackwell's forces began to retreat, their resolve shattered.

Breathing heavily, Danny stood over Blackwell, who glared up at him with hatred. "You think you've won?" Blackwell spat. "This isn't the end."

Danny, his face set with determination, replied, "As long as people like you exist, we'll keep fighting. The engine's power will be used for good, not for greed."

Victor and Evelyn restrained Blackwell, ensuring he couldn't escape. The workshop was secure, and the immediate threat had been thwarted. But they knew this was just one battle in a larger war to protect their discovery and ensure its responsible use.

As they regrouped and tended to their wounds, Danny looked at his allies, his heart filled with gratitude and determination. They had faced a formidable foe and emerged victorious, but their journey was far from over. The ancient steam engine's power held both promise and peril, and it was up to them to navigate the path ahead, standing strong against any who would seek to misuse it.

Evelyn, brushing dust off her sleeves, remarked, "We need to reinforce our defenses and make sure the engine's power is even more secure. Blackwell might be down, but he's not out."

Professor Harkness nodded. "Agreed. And we should continue our research to better understand the engine's capabilities. The more we know, the better prepared we'll be."

Danny took a deep breath, his resolve strengthening. "Let's get to work then. We've got a lot to do."

The team quickly set about reinforcing the workshop's defenses and enhancing the security around the steam engine. Evelyn designed a series of automated turrets powered by the engine's energy, ensuring that any future intrusions would be met with formidable resistance.

Victor, using his military expertise, devised a comprehensive security plan, including strategic placement of guards and surveillance systems. Eleanor and Harkness focused on refining their understanding of the engine's control mechanisms, seeking to improve its stability and efficiency.

Days turned into nights as they worked tirelessly, driven by the urgency of their mission. The workshop buzzed with activity, the air filled with the sounds of clanking metal, hissing steam, and the hum of machinery.

One evening, as the team gathered for a much-needed break, Danny shared his thoughts. "We've made great progress, but we need to stay vigilant. Blackwell isn't the only threat. There are others out there who would seek to exploit this power."

Eleanor nodded in agreement. "We should also think about how we can use the engine's energy to benefit the wider community. If we can harness its power for good, we can show the world its true potential."

Professor Harkness smiled, his eyes twinkling with inspiration. "Indeed. The Pneumarians intended this technology to uplift humanity, not dominate it. We should honor that legacy."

Evelyn's face lit up with excitement. "We could start by using the engine's energy to power the entire village. It would be a great demonstration of its capabilities and a way to improve the lives of the people here."

Victor added, "And it would also show others that this technology can be a force for good, not just a weapon or tool for control."

The idea resonated with the group, and they immediately began planning how to implement it. Danny and Evelyn designed a network to distribute the engine's energy efficiently throughout the village. Professor Harkness and Eleanor worked on public outreach, explaining the benefits of the new technology and garnering community support.

The next few weeks were a flurry of activity. The team installed new energy conduits, powered by the ancient engine, to supply homes, businesses, and public spaces. The villagers watched in awe as streetlights flickered to life, powered by the same mysterious energy that had once only been a legend.

As the project progressed, the villagers' initial skepticism gave way to excitement and gratitude. The reliable and clean energy transformed their lives, making everyday tasks easier and opening new opportunities for growth and innovation. Danny's workshop became a hub of activity, drawing inventors and engineers eager to learn and contribute to the burgeoning technological revolution.

One evening, as the village basked in the glow of its new energy source, Danny stood with his team, overlooking the bustling streets. "Look at what we've achieved together," he said, pride evident in his voice. "This is just the beginning of what we can do."

Evelyn nodded, her eyes scanning the vibrant scene. "It's incredible. But we need to keep pushing the boundaries and finding new ways to use this technology responsibly."

Eleanor added, "We should also continue our research into the Pneumarians' other inventions. There's still so much we don't know, and who knows what other marvels we might uncover?"

As they discussed their next steps, a shadow fell across the workshop entrance. Danny looked up to see a tall figure standing in the doorway, backlit by the evening sun. It was an older man, with a regal bearing and piercing blue eyes.

"Who's there?" Danny called out, stepping forward cautiously.

The man stepped into the light, revealing himself to be an elderly gentleman dressed in finely tailored clothes. He held a walking cane topped with an ornate, carved handle. "Good evening," he said, his voice smooth and commanding. "I am Lord Alistair Blackwood, head of the Royal Society of Engineers. I've come to speak with you about your recent endeavors."

Danny exchanged wary glances with his team. "What brings you here, Lord Blackwood?" he asked, his tone guarded.

Lord Blackwood smiled, his eyes crinkling at the corners. "I've been following your work closely. Your efforts to harness and distribute the power of the ancient steam engine are nothing short of remarkable. The Society is most impressed and wishes to offer its support."

Victor crossed his arms, skeptical. "Support? Or are you here to take control of our work like your namesake, Lord Blackwell?"

Blackwood's smile faded slightly, and he nodded. "I understand your concerns, especially given your recent troubles with my distant cousin, Lord Blackwell. But I assure you, my intentions are quite different. The Royal Society wishes to collaborate, not to commandeer."

Eleanor stepped forward, curious. "Collaborate in what way?"

Blackwood gestured expansively. "We have resources, expertise, and a network of scholars and engineers that could greatly aid your research. In return, we wish to learn from your discoveries and ensure that this technology is used for the benefit of all, in line with the Pneumarians' original vision."

Danny considered Blackwood's offer, his mind racing with possibilities. The support of the Royal Society could accelerate their work and provide the backing they needed to protect their discoveries from future threats.

"What do you think?" he asked his team.

Evelyn was the first to speak. "Having the Royal Society on our side could be invaluable. We'd have access to their resources and a broader platform to share our technology."

Victor nodded in agreement. "As long as we maintain control and ensure that our goals align, it could be a powerful alliance."

Eleanor and Professor Harkness also voiced their support. "The Pneumarians' legacy deserves to be shared and safeguarded," Harkness said. "The Society could help us do that."

Danny turned back to Blackwood. "Very well. We'll consider your offer. But we need to ensure that our work remains true to its purpose and that it's protected from those who would misuse it."

Blackwood nodded, understanding their caution. "Of course. I suggest we begin with a formal agreement outlining our partnership and mutual goals. We can proceed from there."

The next few days were spent negotiating the terms of their collaboration with the Royal Society. Once an agreement was reached, the Society sent a team of engineers and scholars to assist with the ongoing projects. The village became a center of innovation, drawing attention from across the country.

With the combined efforts of Danny's team and the Royal Society, they made rapid progress. New applications for the steam engine's power were developed, from advanced transportation systems to groundbreaking medical devices. The village thrived, becoming a model for what was possible with responsible and innovative use of technology.

However, the increased attention also brought new challenges. Rival industrialists, jealous of their success, began to scheme and plot. Rumors of espionage and sabotage circulated, keeping Danny and his team on high alert.

One evening, while Danny was working late in the workshop, a shadowy figure slipped through a side door, moving silently among the machinery. Danny's instincts, honed by months of vigilance, alerted him to the intruder's presence.

He moved quietly, spotting the figure near the steam engine. "Who's there?" he called out, his voice steady but firm.

The figure froze, then bolted toward the exit. Danny gave chase, his heart pounding. He tackled the intruder just as they reached the door, wrestling them to the ground. With a swift movement, he pulled back the hood of the intruder's cloak, revealing a young woman with determined eyes.

"Who are you?" Danny demanded, still holding her down.

"I'm here to warn you," she said, her voice urgent. "You're in grave danger. Blackwell isn't finished with you. He has powerful allies and they're planning something big."

Danny's grip tightened. "Why should I believe you?"

She looked him straight in the eyes. "Because I was once one of them. My name is Lydia, and I've seen what they're capable of. I've come to help you, but we need to move quickly."

Danny, sensing her sincerity, released his hold and helped her to her feet. "Alright, Lydia. Tell me everything."

As Lydia detailed Blackwell's plans, Danny realized the gravity of the threat they faced. Blackwell had indeed allied with other powerful figures, and they were determined to seize control of the steam engine and its technology.

Danny gathered his team, and together they formulated a plan to counter Blackwell's impending attack. They fortified the workshop and set up a series of traps and defenses. With Lydia's inside knowledge, they were able to anticipate Blackwell's moves and prepare accordingly.

The night of the attack came swiftly. Blackwell's forces approached under the cover of darkness, their intentions clear. But Danny and his allies were ready. As Blackwell's men breached the perimeter, they were met with a barrage of steam-powered traps and defenses, slowing their advance.

Victor led the defense, coordinating their efforts with military precision. Evelyn and the Royal Society engineers worked tirelessly to keep the steam engine running and the defenses powered. Eleanor and Professor Harkness provided support, using their knowledge to outsmart and outmaneuver the attackers.

In the midst of the chaos, Danny and Lydia faced off against Blackwell himself. The confrontation was intense, with Blackwell's rage and determination driving him forward. But Danny, fueled by a fierce resolve to protect their discovery, held his ground.

"You've lost, Blackwell," Danny said, his voice unwavering. "This power will never be yours."

Blackwell sneered, lunging at Danny with a concealed weapon. But Lydia intercepted him, using her knowledge of his tactics to disarm him and deliver a decisive blow.

With Blackwell subdued and his forces in disarray, the tide of the battle turned. Danny's allies rallied, driving the attackers back and securing the workshop once more.

As the dust settled, Danny looked around at his exhausted but victorious team. They had faced incredible odds and emerged stronger, their bond forged in the heat of battle. The steam engine, now more than ever, symbolized hope and progress.

They knew that the challenges were far from over, but they were ready to face whatever came next. With the support of the Royal Society and the unwavering determination of their team, they would continue to protect and develop the Pneumarians' legacy, guiding it toward a future where its immense power could truly benefit all of humanity.

Chapter Eleven: Race Against Time

route. "We'll need to go through the abandoned mines to reach the engine. It's the fastest way, but also the most dangerous."

Professor Harkness adjusted his spectacles, a look of determination on his face. "We must proceed with caution. The mines are known to be unstable, and Blackwell will likely have anticipated our path."

The team set out, their steam-powered carriage chugging along the rugged terrain. The journey to the mines was tense, each member of the group focused on the task ahead. As they neared the entrance, the air grew cooler and the landscape more treacherous.

The entrance to the mines loomed before them, dark and foreboding. Danny took a deep breath. "Everyone ready?"

They nodded in unison, steeling themselves for what lay ahead. They entered the mines, their lanterns casting flickering shadows on the damp, rocky walls. The air was thick with the scent of earth and metal, and the sound of dripping water echoed eerily around them.

As they ventured deeper, they encountered the first of many obstacles. The passage ahead was blocked by a series of large, jagged rocks. Evelyn examined the blockage, her mechanical mind already formulating a solution.

"We can use the portable steam drill to clear this," she said, pulling the device from her pack. "It'll take a few minutes, but it should work."

Danny and Victor helped Evelyn set up the drill. The device roared to life, its powerful engine cutting through the rocks with ease. As they worked, Eleanor kept watch, her keen eyes scanning the darkness for any signs of movement.

With the rocks cleared, they continued their journey. The path wound deeper into the earth, and the air grew colder and more oppressive. Suddenly, a loud crack echoed through the tunnel, and the ground beneath them began to tremble.

"An earthquake?" Eleanor asked, her voice filled with concern.

Professor Harkness shook his head. "No, it's a trap. Blackwell must have rigged the tunnel."

They hurried forward, the tremors growing stronger. Ahead, they saw a large chasm, the ground split open by the vibrations. A makeshift bridge spanned the gap, but it looked unstable.

"We need to cross carefully," Victor said, eyeing the bridge warily. "One at a time, and watch your step."

Danny went first, his heart pounding as he tested each plank. The bridge creaked and swayed, but held firm. He reached the other side and motioned for the others to follow. One by one, they crossed, each step a test of their nerves.

As the last of them reached the other side, the bridge collapsed into the chasm, the wood splintering and crashing into the darkness below. They exchanged relieved glances, knowing they had narrowly escaped disaster.

Their relief was short-lived, however, as they encountered the next obstacle: a series of metal doors, each locked and heavily reinforced. Evelyn examined the locks, her brow furrowed in concentration.

"These are complex mechanisms," she said. "But I can pick them. It'll take some time."

Danny nodded. "Do it. We'll keep watch."

Evelyn set to work, her nimble fingers manipulating the intricate lock mechanisms. As she worked, the rest of the team stood guard, their senses alert for any signs of danger.

Minutes felt like hours as Evelyn painstakingly picked each lock. Finally, with a satisfying click, the last door swung open, revealing a narrow passage that led deeper into the mine.

They moved forward, the air growing colder and more stale. The sound of machinery grew louder, echoing through the tunnels. They were getting closer.

Suddenly, they heard voices ahead. Blackwell's men were just around the corner, preparing for their arrival. Danny signaled for the team to halt, and they quickly formulated a plan.

"We need to take them by surprise," Victor whispered. "Evelyn, can you rig some of our devices to create a distraction?"

Evelyn nodded, pulling out a handful of small, steam-powered gadgets. "Give me a moment."

She set up the devices, positioning them strategically along the tunnel. When she was ready, she activated them, and the tunnel erupted in a cacophony of noise and flashing lights.

Blackwell's men, caught off guard, turned their attention to the distraction. Seizing the opportunity, Danny and his team moved swiftly, taking down the guards with precision and speed. The element of surprise was on their side, and they quickly gained the upper hand.

With the guards subdued, they pressed on. The tunnel widened into a massive chamber, and there, in the center, stood the ancient steam engine. Its brass and steel components glowed with a faint, otherworldly light, and the air hummed with its immense power.

But they were not alone. Lord Blackwell stood beside the engine, his eyes gleaming with triumph. "You're too late, Danny," he sneered. "The engine is mine."

Danny stepped forward, his resolve unwavering. "This engine doesn't belong to you, Blackwell. We won't let you misuse its power."

Blackwell's men closed in, their weapons at the ready. The tension in the chamber was palpable, the air thick with the threat of violence.

Victor, his eyes locked on Blackwell, spoke calmly. "We can end this now, Blackwell. Walk away, and no one gets hurt."

Blackwell laughed, a cold, mirthless sound. "You're in no position to negotiate, Martin. This engine will make me unstoppable."

Danny's team readied themselves for the inevitable confrontation. Eleanor and Professor Harkness moved to the side, their eyes scanning the engine for any way to disable it. Evelyn adjusted her tools, preparing for the fight.

With a signal from Blackwell, his men charged. Danny and Victor met them head-on, their steam-powered weapons clashing in a flurry of sparks and metal. The chamber echoed with the sounds of battle, each clash a test of their determination and skill.

As the fight raged on, Eleanor and Harkness worked to destabilize the engine. They found the control panel and began inputting a series of commands, hoping to shut it down before Blackwell could fully activate it.

Evelyn, using her mechanical expertise, rigged a series of traps and devices to slow down Blackwell's men. Her quick thinking and ingenuity proved invaluable, turning the tide of the battle in their favor.

Danny faced off against Blackwell, their struggle a contest of wills. Blackwell's greed and ambition against Danny's resolve and sense of justice. The two men clashed, their weapons striking with a ferocity born of desperation.

"You can't win, Blackwell," Danny said, his voice steady despite the chaos around them. "This engine is too powerful to be controlled by someone like you."

Blackwell snarled, his eyes blazing with rage. "You underestimate me, Martin. I'll show you what true power looks like."

As the fight reached its climax, Danny managed to disarm Blackwell, sending his weapon clattering to the ground. Seizing the opportunity, he tackled Blackwell, pinning him to the floor.

"Eleanor! Harkness! Now!" Danny shouted.

With a final command input, the engine powered down, its glowing light fading to darkness. The hum of its immense power quieted, leaving the chamber in an eerie silence.

Blackwell, his defeat evident, glared up at Danny. "This isn't over, Martin. I will have that engine."

Danny, breathing heavily, replied, "Not today, Blackwell."

Victor and Evelyn secured Blackwell and his remaining men, ensuring they couldn't cause any more trouble. As the team regrouped, the weight of their victory began to sink in.

"We did it," Eleanor said, her voice filled with relief. "We stopped him."

Professor Harkness nodded, his expression one of pride and exhaustion. "But we must remain vigilant. There will always be those who seek to exploit this power."

Danny looked around at his team, their faces reflecting the trials they had overcome. "We'll keep fighting, together. We've come too far to let anyone take this from us."

With Blackwell and his men subdued, they secured the ancient steam engine, ensuring it would be used for the benefit of all, as the Pneumarians had intended. Their journey was far from over, but they faced the future with newfound strength and determination, ready to protect and develop the incredible legacy they had uncovered.

Chapter Twelve: Personal Revelations

As the team settled back into the workshop, Danny couldn't shake the feeling that there was still so much more to uncover about the ancient steam engine. The recent confrontation with Blackwell had made it clear that understanding the full history and potential of the engine was crucial. One evening, as they gathered around the oak table strewn with manuscripts and artifacts, Danny decided to delve deeper into his family's connection to the engine.

"Eleanor, do you remember the family journals we found earlier?" Danny asked, looking thoughtfully at the stacks of old books and papers. "I think we need to revisit them. There must be more about our ancestors' involvement with the steam engine."

Eleanor nodded, pulling out a particularly old and worn journal. "This one belonged to your great-grandfather, William Martin. We've only scratched the surface of his writings. Let's see what else he left behind."

They began carefully leafing through the journal, the yellowed pages filled with William Martin's meticulous handwriting. It didn't take long before they stumbled upon an entry that caught Danny's attention.

October 12, 1874: _I've discovered something extraordinary. An ancient steam engine, far more advanced than anything we've created. The knowledge contained within this machine is immense, but I fear its power. It must be kept hidden, for in the wrong hands, it could be catastrophic._

Danny read the passage aloud, his voice filled with awe. "He knew about the engine's potential dangers. He understood its power."

Victor, leaning in to look at the journal, added, "It sounds like he took steps to protect it, to ensure it wouldn't be misused."

Evelyn, examining another section of the journal, found more clues. "Here's another entry that mentions a secret society—The Order of the Pneumarians. It says they were dedicated to protecting the steam engine's secrets and ensuring its power was never exploited."

Professor Harkness, intrigued, chimed in. "The Pneumarians were more than just engineers and inventors. They were guardians, tasked with safeguarding this advanced technology."

As they continued to read, they discovered detailed accounts of William Martin's efforts to conceal the engine and its blueprints. He had hidden various components and knowledge across different locations, ensuring that no single person could fully understand or control the engine's power.

November 5, 1875: _I've entrusted parts of the engine and its knowledge to trusted allies within the Order. Each piece is hidden, and only by reuniting them can the engine's full potential be realized. This way, we can prevent its misuse._

Danny's mind raced with the implications. "So there are more hidden components and information out there. If we can find them, we might unlock even more of the engine's capabilities, but we must do so carefully."

Eleanor suggested, "We should follow the clues left by your great-grandfather. If we can locate these hidden pieces, we can ensure they are protected and used responsibly."

The team agreed and decided to start by searching the old Martin family estate. According to the journal, one of the key components was hidden there. They prepared for the journey, gathering supplies and tools they might need to uncover the hidden secrets.

The Martin estate, an imposing manor surrounded by dense woods, had been abandoned for years. Its once-grand halls were now filled with dust and echoes of the past. As they stepped inside, Danny felt a strange sense of connection to his ancestors, knowing they had walked these very halls.

Evelyn led the way to the basement, where they found an old workshop filled with ancient tools and machinery. "This must have been where William did much of his work," she said, her voice hushed with reverence.

They began searching the workshop, looking for any hidden compartments or secret doors. After hours of meticulous examination, Victor discovered a concealed panel behind a dusty bookshelf. With a click, the panel swung open, revealing a hidden room.

Inside, they found a collection of blueprints, journals, and a small, intricately designed box. Danny opened the box, revealing a set of gears and crystals, along with a note in his great-grandfather's handwriting.

To my descendants: _These are the keys to understanding and controlling the steam engine. Use them wisely, and remember that with great power comes great responsibility._

Danny felt a surge of pride and determination. "We've found another piece of the puzzle. This is exactly what we need to continue our work."

Back at the workshop, they carefully examined their findings. The blueprints detailed new ways to harness the engine's power, using the gears and crystals to enhance its stability and efficiency. The journals provided further insights into the Pneumarians' philosophy and methods.

As they integrated these new elements into their research, the steam engine's capabilities began to expand. They were able to generate more power with greater control, opening up new possibilities for innovation.

However, the more they learned, the more they realized the importance of keeping this knowledge safe. Blackwell's defeat had only temporarily halted the threat. Others with less noble intentions would undoubtedly come seeking the engine's power.

Professor Harkness suggested they form their own society, dedicated to continuing the Pneumarians' legacy. "We should gather like-minded individuals who understand the importance of using this technology for the greater good."

Eleanor agreed. "We can protect the engine's secrets while also sharing its benefits with the world, ensuring it's never exploited."

Danny, feeling the weight of his ancestors' legacy on his shoulders, nodded. "We'll call it the New Order of Pneumarians. Together, we'll safeguard this technology and use it to build a better future."

As they worked on formalizing their new society, they continued to uncover more about the steam engine's origins and its immense potential. Each discovery brought them closer to understanding the true power of the engine and the responsibilities that came with it.

One evening, as they were deep in discussion, a coded message arrived, bearing the seal of the original Pneumarians. It was a call for help from a distant city, where rumors of another powerful artifact had surfaced.

Danny read the message aloud, his eyes gleaming with determination. "It looks like our work is far from over. We need to investigate this. If there are more artifacts out there, we must ensure they are protected."

Victor, Evelyn, Eleanor, and Professor Harkness all nodded in agreement. They prepared for their next journey, ready to face whatever challenges lay ahead.

As they set out, Danny couldn't help but feel a deep sense of purpose. His ancestors had begun a mission to protect and harness the power of the steam engine, and now it was up to him and his team to continue that mission. Together, they would navigate the dangers and uncover the secrets of the past, always striving to use their discoveries for the greater good.

Their journey took them to new and uncharted territories, each step filled with peril and promise. Along the way, they encountered allies and enemies, each with their own interest in the ancient technology. The stakes were higher than ever, but Danny and his team were united by a common goal and a shared commitment to protecting the legacy of the Pneumarians.

With each new discovery, they grew stronger and more determined, their bond deepening with every challenge they overcame. The road ahead was fraught with uncertainty, but they knew they were on the path to something truly extraordinary.

Chapter Thirteen: Final Showdown

The tension was palpable as Danny and his team approached the hidden location of the steam engine. The air was thick with anticipation and the weight of their mission. They knew Blackwell would stop at nothing to seize control of the engine's immense power, and the final showdown was inevitable.

The ancient ruins that housed the engine were nestled deep within a secluded valley, surrounded by towering cliffs and dense forests. The journey had been arduous, fraught with traps and obstacles set by Blackwell's forces, but Danny and his team had persevered.

As they approached the entrance, Danny turned to his team, his expression serious. "This is it. Blackwell will be waiting for us. Stay sharp and stick together."

Victor, his steam-powered gauntlets at the ready, nodded. "We've come this far. We can't let him win now."

Evelyn checked her tools and gadgets, her eyes determined. "I've rigged a few surprises of our own. Let's make sure Blackwell regrets ever coming here."

Eleanor and Professor Harkness shared a look of steely resolve. "We're with you, Danny," Eleanor said. "Let's end this."

They entered the ruins, the flickering light from their lanterns casting eerie shadows on the ancient stone walls. The air was cool and damp, and the sound of distant machinery echoed through the passageways. As they ventured deeper, they encountered more of Blackwell's traps—collapsing ceilings, hidden pits, and mechanical guardians. But with Evelyn's expertise and Victor's strength, they overcame each challenge.

Finally, they reached a massive chamber at the heart of the ruins. There, standing before the ancient steam engine, was Lord Blackwell, flanked by his heavily armed guards. The engine loomed behind him, its brass and steel components glowing with a faint, otherworldly light.

Blackwell turned as they entered, his eyes gleaming with triumph. "Danny Martin," he sneered. "I must commend you for making it this far. But this is where your journey ends."

Danny stepped forward, his jaw set. "This engine doesn't belong to you, Blackwell. You'll never control its power."

Blackwell laughed, a cold, mirthless sound. "You still don't understand, do you? This engine is the key to ultimate power, and I will be the one to wield it."

Victor, Evelyn, Eleanor, and Harkness moved to flank Danny, ready for the confrontation. Blackwell's guards raised their weapons, and the room was filled with the tense silence of impending conflict.

With a signal from Blackwell, the guards attacked. The chamber erupted into chaos as steam-powered weapons clashed and the air filled with the sounds of battle. Danny and his team fought valiantly, using their wits and inventions to gain the upper hand.

Victor's gauntlets delivered powerful blows, sending guards sprawling. Evelyn's gadgets created blinding flashes of light and disorienting sounds, giving them a crucial advantage. Eleanor and Harkness provided support, using their knowledge to outmaneuver and outsmart the attackers.

In the midst of the chaos, Danny faced off against Blackwell. The two men circled each other, their eyes locked in a battle of wills.

"You're a fool, Martin," Blackwell spat. "You can't win this fight."

Danny's eyes blazed with determination. "We'll see about that."

Blackwell lunged, his weapon aimed at Danny. But Danny was ready. He dodged the attack and countered with a swift strike, his steam-powered gloves crackling with energy. The two men clashed, their movements a blur of speed and precision.

As they fought, the engine behind them began to hum with increasing intensity. Danny glanced at it, realizing that Blackwell had already started the activation process. If they didn't stop him, the engine's power could be unleashed with devastating consequences.

"Evelyn!" Danny shouted over the din. "We need to shut down the engine!"

Evelyn nodded, understanding the urgency. She and Harkness moved toward the control panel, fighting off guards as they went. Eleanor provided cover, her sharp eyes picking off attackers with precision.

Blackwell, seeing their plan, redoubled his efforts. "You won't stop me, Martin!" he roared, his attacks becoming more frenzied.

But Danny fought with the strength of purpose, his every move driven by the need to protect the engine's power from falling into the wrong hands. He managed to disarm Blackwell, sending his weapon clattering to the ground. With a final, decisive blow, he knocked Blackwell to the floor.

Breathing heavily, Danny stood over his fallen adversary. "It's over, Blackwell. You've lost."

Blackwell, his face twisted with rage, glared up at Danny. "This isn't the end. I will have that engine, one way or another."

Ignoring Blackwell's threats, Danny turned his attention to Evelyn and Harkness, who were working frantically at the control panel. "How's it going?" he called out.

Evelyn looked up, her face determined. "We're almost there. Just a few more adjustments."

The engine's hum grew louder, and the ground beneath them began to shake. Danny felt a surge of panic. They were running out of time.

"Eleanor! Victor! We need to hold them off until Evelyn and Harkness can shut down the engine!" Danny shouted.

Victor and Eleanor nodded, moving to intercept the remaining guards. The battle intensified, the air thick with tension and the acrid smell of steam and metal.

Evelyn's fingers flew over the controls, her mind racing to decode the complex sequences needed to deactivate the engine. Harkness provided support, using his knowledge of the ancient technology to guide her efforts.

Finally, with a triumphant cry, Evelyn pressed a series of buttons, and the engine's hum began to subside. The glowing light faded, and the shaking ground stilled. They had done it.

Danny felt a wave of relief wash over him. They had prevented the engine's power from being unleashed. He looked at his team, their faces reflecting the exhaustion and triumph of their victory.

Blackwell, still on the ground, snarled in defeat. "You may have won this time, Martin, but I will return. And next time, you won't be so lucky."

Danny met Blackwell's gaze with steely resolve. "We'll be ready for you, Blackwell. We'll always be ready."

With the immediate threat neutralized, Danny and his team secured the chamber and ensured that the engine was safely deactivated. They knew that their work was far from over. The engine's power was immense, and its secrets were still largely unknown.

As they left the ruins, the first light of dawn breaking over the horizon, Danny felt a renewed sense of purpose. They had protected the engine and prevented its misuse, but there was still much to learn and many challenges to face.

"We've done it," Eleanor said, her voice filled with a mixture of relief and determination. "But we need to stay vigilant."

Victor nodded. "Blackwell will be back, and others like him. We need to be prepared."

Evelyn, her eyes bright with resolve, added, "And we need to continue our research. There's so much more to discover about this engine and its potential."

Professor Harkness smiled, a look of pride and hope in his eyes. "Together, we can ensure that this technology is used for the greater good. The Pneumarians' legacy is in good hands."

Danny looked at his team, his heart swelling with gratitude and determination. They had faced incredible odds and emerged stronger. Their journey was far from over, but they were united by a common goal and a shared commitment to protecting the incredible legacy they had uncovered.

As they set out on the path ahead, they knew they would face many more challenges. But with their combined skills, knowledge, and resolve, they were ready to navigate the dangers and unlock the full potential of the ancient steam engine, always striving to use their discoveries to build a better future for all.

Chapter Fourteen: Unleashing the Power

The ancient steam engine's hum grew louder, a deep, resonant sound that reverberated through the chamber. Despite Evelyn's efforts, something had gone wrong. A sudden, bright light erupted from the engine, illuminating the entire room and casting eerie shadows on the walls.

Danny's eyes widened in horror as the engine's power surged uncontrollably. "Evelyn, what's happening?"

Evelyn, her face pale with fear, frantically worked the controls. "I don't know! Something's overriding the shutdown sequence. The engine is going into overdrive!"

Blackwell, still restrained but aware of the danger, laughed maniacally. "You've played right into my hands, Martin! The engine's true power is beyond your control!"

Danny felt a cold chill run down his spine. The engine, designed to harness immense energy, was now on the verge of catastrophic overload. If they couldn't contain it, the entire city could be destroyed.

"Eleanor, Harkness, we need to stabilize the engine!" Danny shouted, rushing to Evelyn's side. "Victor, secure Blackwell and get everyone else out of here!"

Victor nodded, dragging Blackwell to the side and ensuring he was firmly restrained. He then turned to help guide the rest of the team to safety, his face set with grim determination.

Eleanor and Professor Harkness joined Danny and Evelyn at the control panel, their minds racing to find a solution. The engine's hum grew deafening, and the ground beneath them shook violently.

"We need to vent the excess energy," Harkness suggested, his voice barely audible over the noise. "If we can redirect it, we might be able to prevent an explosion."

Evelyn nodded, her fingers flying over the controls. "There's an emergency venting system, but it's risky. We could cause a massive steam explosion."

"It's our only chance," Danny said, his voice resolute. "Do it."

Evelyn activated the venting system, and a series of mechanical hisses filled the chamber as steam began to escape through the emergency vents. The pressure eased slightly, but the engine continued to surge with power.

Eleanor, scanning the ancient blueprints, pointed to a secondary control panel. "There's another override system here. If we can activate it, we might be able to stabilize the core."

Danny and Harkness raced to the secondary panel, fighting to keep their balance as the ground shook. They worked together to input the override sequence, their movements precise and desperate.

The engine's light pulsed erratically, casting the chamber in an otherworldly glow. The air crackled with energy, and Danny felt his hair stand on end. They were running out of time.

"Come on, come on," Danny muttered, his fingers trembling as he entered the final commands. "We can do this."

Suddenly, the engine's hum shifted, the pitch changing to a higher, more frantic tone. Evelyn's eyes widened in alarm. "It's still building pressure! We're not venting enough!"

Blackwell, watching from the sidelines, sneered. "You're too late. The engine's power is beyond your comprehension."

Danny refused to give up. "Eleanor, Harkness, help me stabilize the core! Evelyn, keep venting the steam!"

They worked with frantic determination, each second feeling like an eternity. The engine's light grew blinding, and the air was thick with heat and steam.

Finally, with a resounding click, the secondary override system engaged. The engine's hum began to lower, the light dimming slightly. The ground stopped shaking, and the pressure eased.

"We did it," Danny whispered, barely able to believe it. "We stabilized it."

But their relief was short-lived. A loud, ominous crack echoed through the chamber as a fissure opened in the engine's core. The power they had contained was now leaking, threatening to unleash its full destructive force.

"We need to seal that fissure," Evelyn said urgently. "If we don't, the core will rupture, and the city will be lost."

Danny looked around desperately. "We need something strong enough to withstand the pressure."

Eleanor's eyes lit up with an idea. "The crystals! They're designed to handle immense energy. If we can place them around the fissure, they might contain the leak."

Victor, hearing the plan, rushed over with the crystals they had brought. "Here, use these!"

Danny, Evelyn, Eleanor, and Harkness worked together to position the crystals around the fissure. The engine's light flickered, and the air hummed with energy as they carefully placed each crystal, creating a barrier to contain the leak.

The pressure continued to build, but the crystals began to glow, absorbing the excess energy. Slowly, the engine's hum stabilized, and the fissure stopped expanding.

"We're doing it," Evelyn said, her voice filled with hope. "The crystals are holding!"

The team worked tirelessly, reinforcing the barrier and ensuring the engine remained stable. The ground was no longer shaking, and the air felt cooler as the excess steam vented safely.

Finally, after what felt like an eternity, the engine's light returned to a soft, steady glow. The hum was a gentle, rhythmic pulse, and the chamber was filled with a sense of calm.

Danny stepped back, his body trembling with exhaustion. "We did it. We contained the engine."

Blackwell, now looking defeated, slumped against the wall. "You may have won this battle, Martin, but the war is far from over."

Danny turned to his team, their faces reflecting a mixture of relief and determination. "We'll always be ready to protect this engine and its power. Together, we can ensure it's used for the greater good."

As they secured the chamber and made plans to safeguard the engine, Danny knew their journey was far from over. The engine's true power had been revealed, and the responsibility to protect and harness it for the benefit of all weighed heavily on his shoulders.

But with his team by his side and the legacy of the Pneumarians guiding them, Danny felt ready to face whatever challenges lay ahead.

Chapter Fifteen: Resolution of Conflict

The tension in the chamber was almost unbearable as the team worked to stabilize the ancient steam engine. With the crystals now absorbing the excess energy, the engine's power began to settle. Danny, Evelyn, Eleanor, Victor, and Professor Harkness moved quickly and efficiently, each playing their part to ensure the engine was safely contained.

Danny stood before the main control panel, his hands flying over the ancient controls. "We need to synchronize the energy output with the containment fields. If we can do that, we can prevent any further surges."

Evelyn, working beside him, adjusted the settings on the emergency venting system. "I've rerouted the excess steam to the secondary vents. That should help manage the pressure."

Eleanor and Professor Harkness monitored the crystal containment field, ensuring that it remained stable and effective. "The crystals are holding, but we need to maintain a steady flow of energy to keep them from overheating," Harkness observed.

Victor, standing guard, kept a wary eye on Blackwell, who remained restrained and sullen. "I'll make sure he doesn't cause any more trouble," Victor said grimly.

As they worked, the engine's light continued to pulse gently, a far cry from the chaotic surge of power that had threatened to destroy everything. Danny's fingers moved with practiced precision, inputting commands and adjusting settings. Gradually, the hum of the engine evened out, becoming a steady, controlled rhythm.

"We're getting there," Danny said, his voice tense but hopeful. "Just a bit more and we'll have it fully stabilized."

Evelyn nodded, her eyes fixed on the readouts. "The pressure is dropping, and the energy levels are normalizing. Keep it up, Danny."

With a final, deliberate series of inputs, Danny initiated the synchronization sequence. The engine's light flickered once, then settled into a soft, stable glow. The hum became a gentle, rhythmic pulse, indicating that the engine was now fully under control.

Danny stepped back, taking a deep breath. "We've done it. The engine is stable."

A collective sigh of relief swept through the team. Eleanor and Harkness checked the containment field one last time, ensuring that everything was secure. Victor relaxed his stance slightly, but remained vigilant.

Evelyn turned to Danny, a smile breaking through her exhaustion. "We did it. We really did it."

Danny nodded, feeling the weight of their accomplishment. "Yes, we did. But we need to make sure it stays this way. We can't let anyone, especially Blackwell, get their hands on this technology."

Blackwell, his face twisted with defeat and anger, spat out, "You think you've won? This is just a temporary victory. The engine's power will be mine."

Danny met Blackwell's gaze with steely determination. "Not as long as we're here to protect it. You've seen what this engine can do, and you've seen that we're capable of controlling it. Leave now, and never come back."

Victor tightened his grip on Blackwell's restraints. "Let's get him out of here and hand him over to the authorities. He's done enough damage."

As they escorted Blackwell out of the chamber, Danny took a moment to reflect on everything they had been through. They had faced incredible odds, and yet they had managed to regain control of one of the most powerful pieces of technology ever created. The responsibility of safeguarding the steam engine and its secrets was immense, but Danny knew they were up to the task.

Back in the workshop, the team regrouped and assessed their next steps. They needed to fortify their defenses, continue their research, and ensure that the engine was used responsibly.

Eleanor spoke up, her voice filled with determination. "We should establish a secure facility where we can continue our work without the constant threat of intrusion. A place where we can study the engine and its technology safely."

Professor Harkness agreed. "And we should build alliances with other like-minded individuals and organizations. The more support we have, the better we can protect and develop this technology."

Evelyn added, "We should also document everything we've learned and create a comprehensive guide to the engine. That way, future generations will have the knowledge they need to continue our work."

Danny nodded, feeling a renewed sense of purpose. "Let's get to it. We have a lot of work ahead of us, but I know we can do it. Together, we'll ensure that this engine is used for the greater good."

As they set to work, Danny couldn't help but feel a deep connection to his ancestors and the Pneumarians who had started this journey centuries ago. They had entrusted him with an incredible legacy, and he was determined to honor that trust.

Days turned into weeks as they established their new facility, a secure and well-fortified compound designed to protect the steam engine and its secrets. They continued their research, uncovering new facets of the engine's capabilities and developing innovative applications for its energy.

Their efforts began to bear fruit as they shared their discoveries with the world, demonstrating the positive potential of the steam engine's power. Communities benefited from clean, reliable energy, and new technologies emerged that improved lives and fostered progress.

Despite their success, they remained vigilant. The threat of those who would misuse the engine's power was ever-present, but Danny and his team were prepared. They had faced the worst and emerged stronger, their bond unbreakable and their resolve unwavering.

As they looked to the future, they knew that their journey was far from over. The ancient steam engine held many more secrets, and the challenges ahead would test their ingenuity and determination.

Chapter Sixteen: Blackwell's Downfall

The team worked quickly to secure Blackwell and his remaining loyalists, binding them with sturdy ropes and confiscating their weapons. Victor took the lead in escorting Blackwell out of the chamber, keeping a firm grip on his arm. As they made their way through the ancient ruins, the team could feel the tension easing, the immediate threat of the engine's catastrophic power finally under control.

Outside the ruins, the city guards, alerted by the chaos and explosions from the confrontation, arrived in force. They quickly took Blackwell and his men into custody, securing the perimeter and ensuring that the area was safe.

A high-ranking officer approached Danny and his team. "We received reports of an imminent threat. It looks like you've managed to avert a disaster. What happened here?"

Danny briefly explained the situation, highlighting Blackwell's attempted seizure of the ancient steam engine and the potential catastrophe they had narrowly avoided. The officer nodded, understanding the gravity of the situation.

"Lord Blackwell will face justice for his actions," the officer said firmly. "We'll ensure he's held accountable."

Blackwell, now subdued and flanked by guards, glared at Danny with a mixture of hatred and resignation. "This isn't over, Martin. You may have won today, but there will always be those who seek power."

Danny met his gaze with calm determination. "And we'll be here to stop them. Every time."

With Blackwell and his men apprehended, the city guards escorted them away, and the atmosphere in the ruins lightened. The sense of danger that had hung over them dissipated, replaced by a feeling of relief and accomplishment.

Eleanor turned to Danny, her face reflecting the collective sentiment of the team. "We did it. We stopped him and saved the city."

Victor, still keeping a wary eye on the departing prisoners, nodded. "But we need to stay vigilant. There will always be others like Blackwell."

Evelyn, her mechanical mind already working on new security measures, added, "We should reinforce our defenses and ensure the engine is protected. We can't let this happen again."

Professor Harkness, adjusting his spectacles, looked thoughtfully at the ancient ruins. "And we must continue our research. The more we understand about the engine, the better we can safeguard its power."

The team agreed and set about their tasks with renewed purpose. Back at their workshop, they fortified their defenses, implementing advanced security systems and monitoring protocols to ensure the engine remained safe. They also reached out to trusted allies within the scientific and engineering communities, forming a network dedicated to protecting and responsibly using the steam engine's technology.

Meanwhile, the city began to recover from the recent turmoil. The successful containment of the engine's power and the apprehension of Blackwell brought a sense of peace and stability. The community, inspired by Danny and his team's efforts, rallied together to support their ongoing work.

Danny, Evelyn, Eleanor, Victor, and Professor Harkness continued their research, delving deeper into the engine's capabilities and exploring new applications for its energy. They documented their findings meticulously, creating a comprehensive archive to guide future generations.

One evening, as they gathered around the oak table in their fortified workshop, Danny reflected on their journey. "We've come a long way, but there's still so much to do. The engine's power is incredible, but we must always remember the responsibility that comes with it."

Eleanor nodded, her eyes filled with determination. "We must ensure that this technology is used for the greater good, just as the Pneumarians intended."

Victor, ever the protector, added, "And we must remain vigilant. There will always be those who seek to misuse this power, but we'll be ready to face them."

Evelyn, her hands busy with a new invention, smiled. "We've proven that we can handle whatever comes our way. As long as we stick together, we can overcome any challenge."

Professor Harkness, his voice filled with pride, concluded, "The legacy of the Pneumarians is in good hands. Our work will ensure that their vision of a better future becomes a reality."

As they continued their work, Danny and his team remained steadfast in their commitment to protecting and advancing the steam engine's technology. They knew that the road ahead would be filled with challenges, but their resolve was unbreakable.

Their efforts began to bear fruit as they developed new innovations powered by the engine's energy. The city, now a hub of technological advancement, flourished. Clean, reliable energy transformed daily life, and new inventions improved health, transportation, and communication.

Despite their successes, they never lost sight of the engine's potential dangers. They established strict guidelines and safety protocols, ensuring that their discoveries were used responsibly. Their network of allies grew, and the New Order of Pneumarians became a respected organization dedicated to ethical innovation.

As the years passed, Danny and his team became mentors and leaders in the field of steam technology. Their workshops became centers of learning and creativity, attracting brilliant minds from around the world. Together, they worked to unlock the full potential of the ancient steam engine, always guided by the principles of responsibility and progress.

Their journey was far from over, but they faced the future with confidence and determination. The ancient steam engine, once a source of danger and uncertainty, had become a beacon of hope and innovation. Danny and his team, united by their shared commitment, were ready to navigate whatever challenges lay ahead, always striving to use their discoveries to build a better future for all.

Epilogue

The sun was setting over the bustling city, casting a warm golden light across the rooftops and illuminating the spires and smokestacks that had become a symbol of the new era of innovation. From the top floor of their fortified workshop, Danny stood by a large window, gazing out at the transformed skyline. The journey he had embarked on had been long and fraught with challenges, but as he reflected on the past months, he felt a deep sense of fulfillment and purpose.

Behind him, the workshop buzzed with activity. His friends and allies—Evelyn, Eleanor, Victor, and Professor Harkness—were engrossed in their latest projects, each contributing their unique skills to the ongoing mission of harnessing the steam engine's power for the greater good.

Danny's thoughts drifted back to the beginning of their adventure. He remembered the first time he had discovered the ancient steam engine and the mysteries it held. He thought about the revelations regarding his ancestors, the Pneumarians, and their role in creating and protecting this incredible technology. The responsibility of safeguarding and advancing their legacy weighed heavily on him, but he had embraced it with unwavering resolve.

Eleanor approached him, her face reflecting the same sense of pride and accomplishment. "It's amazing to see how far we've come, isn't it?"

Danny nodded, his gaze still on the horizon. "Yes, it is. We've faced so many obstacles, but we've also achieved so much. The city is thriving, and our work is making a real difference."

Victor joined them, his expression serious yet content. "And we've managed to keep the engine safe from those who would misuse it. Blackwell's defeat was a turning point, but we have to stay vigilant."

Evelyn, her hands covered in grease from working on a new invention, chimed in. "We've built something incredible here. And there's still so much more we can do. The possibilities are endless."

Professor Harkness, always the voice of wisdom, added, "The key is to continue learning and innovating while remembering the responsibilities that come with such power. The Pneumarians understood that, and we must too."

Danny turned to face his friends, his heart swelling with gratitude. "We couldn't have done any of this without each other. We've become more than just a team—we're a family. And I'm grateful for every one of you."

They smiled, sharing a moment of quiet camaraderie. The bond they had forged through their shared struggles and triumphs was unbreakable, and it gave Danny the strength to face whatever the future might hold.

As the sun dipped below the horizon, casting the city in a twilight glow, Danny thought about the journey ahead. There were still many mysteries to uncover, new challenges to overcome, and endless possibilities to explore. The ancient steam engine, with all its potential, was just the beginning.

"We have a lot of work ahead of us," Danny said, his voice filled with determination. "But I know we can handle it. Together, we'll continue to innovate and protect our city. And who knows what other adventures await us?"

Evelyn grinned, wiping her hands on a rag. "I'm ready for anything. Bring it on."

Eleanor nodded in agreement. "Whatever comes our way, we'll face it together."

Victor, ever the protector, added, "And we'll ensure that the engine's power is used for good. Always."

Professor Harkness smiled, a twinkle in his eye. "The future is ours to shape. Let's make it a bright one."

As they stood together, looking out over the city they had helped to transform, Danny felt a profound sense of hope and possibility. The journey had been challenging, but it had also been incredibly rewarding. And with his friends by his side, he knew that they could face anything the future might hold.

The city below buzzed with life and energy, a testament to their hard work and dedication. Steam-powered vehicles moved through the streets, lights flickered on in homes and businesses, and the air was filled with the hum of progress. It was a new era, built on the foundations of the past but looking boldly towards the future.

Danny turned back to the workshop, ready to dive into their next project. There was always more to discover, more to create, and more to protect. The legacy of the Pneumarians lived on through their efforts, and he was determined to honor that legacy every step of the way.

As they resumed their work, the sense of excitement and possibility was palpable. The adventures they had experienced were just the beginning, and Danny knew that there were many more to come. Together, they would continue to push the boundaries of innovation, harness the power of the ancient steam engine, and build a future that honored the past while embracing the potential of tomorrow.

The journey was far from over, but with his newfound family by his side, Danny was ready for whatever lay ahead. The city was safe, the engine was secure, and the future was filled with endless possibilities. And with each new discovery, they would continue to forge a legacy of hope, progress, and responsibility, always striving to use their knowledge and power for the greater good.

www.ingramcontent.com/pod-product-compliance
Lightning Source LLC
Chambersburg PA
CBHW081237130726
47997CB00009B/2898